"I'm going to wa

Jesse raised his eyebrows

"You heard me. I'm dre_____ is a dream. It has to be. I am definitely not standing on a ledge halfway up a mountain, talking to a man who— who looks as if he stepped out of Central Casting for a movie starring John Wayne." A curl of golden brown hair blew over her lip; she shoved it behind her ear and her chin rose a little higher. "John Wayne is dead, and I am dreaming. End of story."

Jesse almost laughed. She was a tough piece of work. Whatever else she was, he had to admire her for that.

"I've got news for you, baby. John Wayne's alive. And this is no dream."

"Wrong on both counts," she said. If her chin went up any higher, she'd tumble over backward. "John Wayne is history. And I am sound asleep in my tent. There's not a way in the world you can make me think otherwise." Her eyes—more violet than ever—narrowed. "This is not real."

"You're wasting valuable time. The descent's going to be tough enough without factoring in the heat."

"No," she said, though now there was a faint quaver in her voice, "I told you, this isn't real."

"It damned well is," Jesse snarled, and he proved it by pulling her into his arms, bending his head and covering her mouth with his.

Mills & Boon® Modern™ Romance is pleased to present this new and exciting mini-series!

MEN WITHOUT MERCY

Arrogant and proud, unashamedly male!

Modern™ Romance with a retro twist…

Step back in time to when men were men— and women knew just how to tame them!

This month:

BLACKWOLF'S REDEMPTION by Sandra Marton

Experience the drama, excitement and passion when an independent twenty-first century woman is thrown back in time and comes face to face with a twentieth-century man as arrogant as he is gorgeous and as confident as he is sexy…

Sparks fly and temperatures soar!

BLACKWOLF'S REDEMPTION

BY
SANDRA MARTON

First published in Great Britain 2010
Harlequin Mills & Boon Limited,
Eton House, 18-24 Paradise Road, Richmond, Surrey TW9 1SR

© Sandra Myles 2010

ISBN: 978 0 263 87794 6

Harlequin Mills & Boon policy is to use papers that are natural, renewable and recyclable products and made from wood grown in sustainable forests. The logging and manufacturing process conform to the legal environmental regulations of the country of origin.

Printed and bound in Spain
by Litografia Rosés, S.A., Barcelona

Sandra Marton wrote her first novel while she was still in primary school. Her doting parents told her she'd be a writer some day, and Sandra believed them. In secondary school and college she wrote dark poetry nobody but her boyfriend understood—though, looking back, she suspects he was just being kind. As a wife and mother she wrote murky short stories in what little spare time she could manage, but not even her boyfriend-turned-husband could pretend to understand those. Sandra tried her hand at other things, among them teaching and serving on the Board of Education in her home town, but the dream of becoming a writer was always in her heart.

At last Sandra realised she wanted to write books about what all women hope to find: love with that one special man, love that's rich with fire and passion, love that lasts for ever. She wrote a novel, her very first, and sold it to Mills & Boon® Modern™ Romance. Since then she's written more than sixty books, all of them featuring sexy, gorgeous, larger-than-life heroes. A four-time RITA® award finalist, she's also received five *RT Book Reviews* awards, and has been honoured with RT's Career Achievement Award for Series Romance. Sandra lives with her very own sexy, gorgeous, larger-than-life hero in a sun-filled house on a quiet country lane in the north-eastern United States.

'Reality is merely an illusion,
albeit a very persistent one.'
Albert Einstein, commenting on our perceptions

'And now for something completely different.'
*'Monty Python's Flying Circus',
commenting on that very same subject*

CHAPTER ONE

Blackwolf Canyon, Montana, 5:34 a.m.,
one hour before the summer solstice, June 21, 2010

THE moon had set almost five hours ago. Still, night clung tenaciously to the land.

The high, rocky walls of the canyon seemed determined to hold to the chill of darkness; a razor-sharp wind swept down from the surrounding peaks and whipped through the scrub, its eerie sigh all that disturbed the silence.

Sienna Cummings shivered.

There was a wildness to this place, but in these last moments before the dawn light pierced the bottom of the canyon, she could almost sense the land's ancient, often bloody history.

A heavy arm wrapped around her shoulders.

"Here," Jack Burden said, "let me warm you up."

Sienna forced a smile and stepped free of the expedition leader's embrace.

"I'm fine," she said politely. "Just excited. About the solstice," she added quickly, before Burden could pull his usual trick of turning whatever she said into a suggestive remark.

No such luck.

"I'm excited, too," he said, managing to do it, anyway. "Lucky me. Alone with you, in the dark."

They were hardly alone. There were four others with them: two graduate students, an associate professor from the Anthropology Department and a girl Burden had described as his secretary. From the way she looked at him, Sienna doubted if that was her real job, but that was fine with her; for the most part, it kept her obnoxious boss from sniffing after her.

Except at certain moments.

Like right now.

Never mind that they were about to view something remarkable. That soon, the sun's light would be visible between the huge slabs of rock a third of the way up Blackwolf Mountain. That a shaft of that light would stream down and illuminate a circle some holy man had inscribed on a sacred stone thousands of years ago. Never mind that this would be the first summer solstice in decades that outsiders had been allowed in the canyon at all, or that everything here was about to change because the land was about to be sold to a developer.

All Jack Burden could think of was seducing her.

Yes, there were laws against sexual harassment. All she had to do was file a complaint with the university—and then live with the knowledge that her career would stall. It was the twenty-first century, women were the legal equals of men….

But in some of the ways that counted most, nothing had changed.

Some men still thought it was their right to take what they wanted, especially when it came to women.

"It's almost time," one of the grad students said breathlessly.

Sienna drew her thoughts together and focused on the jagged peak ahead of them. Half an hour, was more like it, but the waiting was part of the experience. She'd been on lots of ancient sites; she'd seen the summer sun rise at Chaco Canyon, traced the glyphs on the great temple at Chichén Itzá. One magical night, she'd been permitted to walk among the monoliths at Stonehenge.

And yet, there was something special about this place.

She could feel it. In her bones. In her heart. She would never say such a thing to anyone—she was a scientist, and science scoffed at what people claimed to feel in their bones. Still, there was something special here. About this night. About being here.

She must have made a little sound. A whisper. An indrawn breath, because Jack Burden leaned toward her.

"Aren't you glad I brought you with me?" he said.

He made it sound like a gift, but it wasn't. Sienna was months away from her doctorate; she had studied Blackwolf Canyon for two years. She had earned her place on this expedition. She knew everything about the canyon, from the ancients who had settled it, to the Comanche and Sioux warriors who had fought for it, to its mysterious last-known owner, Jesse Blackwolf, though what had become of him was uncertain.

He, too, had been a warrior. He'd fought in Vietnam a decade before she was born, returned home in what should have been triumph—and virtually disappeared.

She'd tried to find out what had become of him, telling herself it had to do with her studies, her thesis, but it wasn't true. The man had captured her imagination. Ridiculous, of course. Cultural anthropologists studied cultures, not individuals. But there was something about Jesse Blackwolf….

"Here it comes," one of the grad students yelled. "Just another couple of minutes!"

Sienna nodded, wrapped her arms around herself and waited.

Blackwolf Canyon, Montana, 5:34 a.m., one hour before the summer solstice, June 22, 1975

Jesse Blackwolf's horse shifted impatiently beneath him.

"Soon," Jesse said softly, stroking a calloused hand along the animal's satiny neck.

Eyes narrowed, Jesse looked at the jagged peak ahead of him.

Half an hour, and he could ride out of this place and never look back.

His ancestors had come here to celebrate their gods. He had come to say goodbye to them. There was no room in his life for nonsense.

He hadn't planned on this final visit. What for? A summer solstice was a summer solstice. The earth reached the top of its northernmost tilt and that was that.

His ancestors had figured it out and they'd venerated the process. They'd made a big thing out of these final minutes that marked the start of the longest stretch of daylight in the year.

Not him.

It wasn't belief in superstition that had brought Jesse here. On the contrary. It was disbelief. Looking at this foolishness as it happened seemed vital. He'd accepted it as a boy but he was a long way from boyhood. He was a man, older and wiser than the first time he'd ridden out to view the solstice.

The big gray stallion snorted softly. Jesse's hard, chiseled mouth turned up in what might almost have been a smile.

"Okay," he said, "maybe you're right. Older? Absolutely. Wiser? Who knows."

The horse snorted again and tossed his massive head as if to say, *What are we doing out here when we both should be sleeping?* Jesse couldn't fault the animal for that. Trouble was that an hour ago, he'd awakened from a fitful sleep, taken

Cloud from the warmth of his stall, slipped a bridle over his head and obeyed the sudden impulse to ride out to the canyon and watch the sunrise.

Damn it, Jesse told himself coldly, *be honest!*

He was here by plan, by design, by the need to sever, once and for all, whatever ties remained between him and the old ways.

Impulse had nothing to do with it.

He'd known that the solstice was coming. You didn't have to be part Comanche and Sioux for that. His mother's Anglo blood was more than sufficient. So were the three wasted years he'd spent at university. The sun reached a certain declination, a certain height and angle in the sky, and twice a year, you had a solstice.

Solstices were real.

It was the god myths that were bull.

The stuff about the renewal of the earth, of the spirit. The nonsense about what it meant to a warrior to be on this very spot at the moment the sun rose behind the jagged peaks of Blackwolf Mountain, shone its light between the two enormous stony slabs on the rocky shelf some forty feet above the ground, then centered on the spiral the Old Ones had etched into the horizontal stone between them.

The idiocy about how viewing this particular rising sun could change a man's life forever.

Jesse gave a bitter laugh.

His father had believed in all of it, as had his grandfather, his great-grandfather and, most probably, every Blackwolf warrior whose DNA he'd inherited.

For most of his thirty years, he'd believed in it, too. Not all of it—a twentieth-century man with the better part of a university degree under his belt wasn't about to buy into mythology.

What he *had* believed in was respecting the old ways. Respecting the continuity of tradition. And, yes, he'd even believed in honoring, if only a little, events like the solstices.

What harm could there be, even if a man knew the scientific reasons for why such things occurred?

His father had brought him to this place when he was twelve.

"Soon the sun will rise," he had said, "and the light of time past and time yet to come will fall on the sacred circle. The vows a man takes at the summer solstice will determine his true path forever. Are you ready to make a vow, my son?"

At that age, Jesse's head and heart had brimmed with stories of his warrior ancestors. His father had told those tales to him all his life; his mother—born in the East, to parents who had never met an Indian until they met their new son-in-law—had read them to him from the children's books she wrote and illustrated.

And so, of course, Jesse had been ready.

As soon as the sun began its slow rise into the heavens, he'd tilted his face to its light, arms outstretched, hands open and cupped to receive its gift of brilliance and warmth, and he'd offered himself, everything he was, to the spirit of the warriors who had gone before him.

His father had smiled with pride. His mother, told of his vow when he and his father rode home, had hugged him. Even as he grew older and slowly began to understand that the old stories were just stories and nothing more, he'd been glad he'd made the vow, glad his father had included him in this ancient tradition.

But by the time Jesse was in college, everything seemed changed. There was a war taking place in a distant land. Boys he'd grown up with were dying in it. He would not be drafted; college kids were not going to be put in harm's way.

It seemed wrong. He was descended from warriors. What was he doing, hiding away in stuffy classrooms at a university where some had taken to ridiculing everything he believed?

At twenty, Jesse knew it was time to honor the vow he'd made when he was twelve.

He left college. Enlisted in the army. His father had been proud of him. His mother had wept. He went through basic training, was plucked from the others and offered the chance to become part of an elite group called Special Forces. He served with honorable men in what he thought was an honorable cause....

And watched everything he'd believed in turn to dust.

Cloud whinnied and pawed the ground. Jesse blinked, brought his thoughts back where they belonged, to this place where it had all begun, his descent into a way of life that had deceived him.

The solstice was starting.

The sky had taken on that faint purple light that marks the end of night as the sunlight began to fall on the mountain. Light filled the narrow space between the two great slabs of rocks placed there by his ancestors thousands of years ago.

The sun rose higher.

Jesse drew a deep breath.

The last time he'd sat a horse in this place, he'd been filled with childish idealism. Not anymore. He was a man, with a man's knowledge of the world. He had lost everything: his father to cancer, his mother to despair only months later, his own honor to a war that had been a sham.

So, yes. He would make another vow here as the sun rose. He would vow to rid the world of superstition. He would sell the canyon, sell his thousands of acres, and if some ambitious snake-oil salesman decided to charge admission to view the solstice or the equinox or the moon-rise, let him.

He had already put a stop to the age-old tradition of permitting his people to ride here to view what they considered a sacred rite. Men—boys, especially—should not be taught to put their faith in things that could someday make a mockery of their beliefs.

This was a place of lies and ignorance. It was time to put a stop to it.

The sale papers were already on his desk. He would sign them, courier them to his attorney, and all this nonsense would be—

Cloud whinnied. Jesse looked straight ahead at the beam of bright sunlight beginning to slip between the two slabs of stone.

He drew an unsteady breath. His pulse was racing; he felt light-headed. Damn it, superstition could be a powerful—

What in hell was that?

He'd expected the shaft of light to fall on the so-called sacred stone. One thing about science: once you understood it, you could count on it to perform the necessary parlor tricks.

But what was that other light? That sudden green zigzag overhead?

There it was again. An electric bolt of color that shattered the sky.

His horse danced backward, shying with fear. Jesse grasped the reins in his right hand more tightly, murmured words of assurance to the horse.

To himself.

Lightning, in a clear dawn sky? Lightning without thunder? Lightning the color of emeralds? The weather could be unpredictable here. This was northern Montana, after all, a place of mountains and valleys and…

"Damn!"

Another streak of lightning sizzled through the sky behind the jagged peak. The sun vanished; darkness covered the land. Cloud rose on his hind legs and pawed the air, crying out with fear. Jesse fought to calm the agitated animal.

The sky lit again. Green lightning flashed between the stone slabs and pulsed at the heart of the sacred circle.

The stallion went crazy, screaming, trying to throw Jesse to the ground.

The breath caught in Jessie's throat.

The lightning had stopped.

The darkness vanished.

The sun appeared, a bright yellow ball against a clear blue sky.

It lit the canyon, the peaks, the tenacious shrubs and lodge-pole pines that clung to the inhospitable slope before him, but Jesse had eyes for only one thing.

A figure. A human figure that lay, still as death, in the very center of the sacred stone.

CHAPTER TWO

THE climb to the ledge was as tricky and dangerous as Jesse remembered, more like sixty feet instead of forty because of all the maneuvering necessary to find the right hand and footholds, and the rush of adrenaline pumping through him didn't help. He could feel his muscles tensing.

Jesse stopped, counted to ten, took half a dozen deep breaths as the sweat poured off his tanned skin. If he fell, then there'd be two of them for the vultures to pick over.

Two of what? his brain said. Had he actually seen somebody up there?

Hell. There was no time for that. He had to keep moving.

The ledge was right above him now. This was the trickiest part; he'd have to lean back with nothing behind him but air to get a decent handhold. Wouldn't it be a bitch if he'd gone through all this nonsense and the thing lying on the stone wasn't human at all? There was lots of wildlife here. Elk, deer, but neither of those could have scrambled up this high. A wolf? No, again. A bear, maybe. Or a mountain lion.

He might have made this climb just for a look at the carcass of a dead animal. Or an injured one. Hunters might have ignored his No Trespassing signs. Nobody from around here. They knew better. But an outsider…

For God's sake, you've seen what some of those idiots who call themselves hunters can do.

Why hadn't he thought of that sooner?

A wounded grizzly would be a hell of a thing to find. Well, it was too late to worry about that now. Jesse took a deep breath. One last pull with the powerful muscles of his arms and shoulders and he hoisted himself up on the narrowest part of the ledge.

His heart caught in his throat.

There was something here, all right. And it wasn't an animal. It was a woman.

She was unconscious but alive; her face was white as a fish's belly but he could see the faint rise and fall of her breasts.

A moan rose from her throat. She didn't have any obvious wounds, but that didn't mean anything. For all he knew, she might have been struck by that strange lightning. Lightning was dangerous. It might have damaged her heart. Or she might have hit her head and suffered a concussion.

He had no way of knowing her condition.

He told himself she deserved whatever had happened to her. Outsiders had no business here. Still, instinct took over. He had been trained to save lives, as well as take them. He knelt down beside her and took a closer look.

She wasn't shivering. That was good. He touched his hand to the side of her neck. Her skin was warm. That was good, too. He could see her pulse beating—hell, racing—in her throat.

He put his hand over her heart.

Its beat was strong and steady…and her breast filled his palm. He jerked his hand away and sat back on his heels.

"Wake up," he said sharply.

She didn't move.

"Come on, open your eyes."

She moaned again. Her lashes lifted, revealing irises the color of spring violets.

"Are you injured? Does anything hurt?"

The tip of her tongue came out and swept lightly over her lips. She was looking at him, but he doubted if she could really see him; her eyes were blurry.

"Concentrate," he said coldly. "Listen to what I'm saying. Are you hurt?"

Her gaze sharpened; her eyes seemed to darken. Her lips parted.

"That's it. Look at me and tell me if anything—"

"Oh, my God," she gasped.

And then her mouth opened wide and her scream echoed and reechoed through the silence of the canyon.

The scream that erupted from Sienna's throat was high and thin and filled with terror, but sheer, unadulterated terror was precisely what she felt.

A man was bending over her. He had the painted face of a savage, with black stripes delineating the sharpness of his high cheekbones. His hair was black, too, and long, held back with a strip of something, maybe deer hide. Her eyes dropped lower. An eagle's talon was hung around his neck, dangling from a narrower length of leather.

Dangling against his—*oh, God*—his naked, tautly muscled chest.

Fear beat gauzy wings in her blood. There was only one explanation. A lunatic was wandering the Montana high country and she'd run straight into him.

Don't scream again, she told herself. *Do not scream again. Be calm, be calm, be—*

"Get away from me!" she shrieked as he leaned toward her. She dug her elbows into the unyielding surface beneath her and tried desperately to scramble backward. No way. The man put his big, hard hands on her shoulders and shoved her down.

"Don't move."

His voice was low and rough, and now she was sure he was crazy. Don't move? Of course she was going to move. She was going to run like the wind, but first she had to get free of his hands.

"I said don't move," he growled. "Or I'll have to restrain you."

Restrain? What kind of madman used a word like *restrain?* And wasn't he already doing that? Questions tumbled through her head. Who was this nut? Where had he come from? For that matter, where was she? Her gaze flew past him, to the mountain that loomed over her, and beyond it, to the blazing sun.

The sun. The solstice.

That was it. The solstice. She'd been observing it, waiting for the moment the new summer sun would send a dagger of light between the standing slabs that guarded the sacred stone and then, without warning, lightning had torn apart the sky. Green lightning, zigzagging between the stones.

A black void had opened before her. She'd felt herself falling into it, spinning inside it....

And then, nothing. A nothing so cold, intense and empty she'd felt as if her bones might become petrified, as if the emptiness would swallow her.

But it hadn't, because she was here, with a man she'd never seen before crouched beside her. A savage with a hard face, eyes as cold and black as obsidian, and a mouth as thin as the slash of a rapier.

Sienna tried to swallow. Impossible. Terror had leeched the

moisture from her mouth. The man watched the motion of her throat, then lifted his eyes to her face again.

"Are you hurt?"

Was she? Carefully, she flexed her fingers, her toes, her back.

"I don't—"

"Do you ache anywhere?"

Why would he care? Still, her response was automatic. "My head."

One hand left her shoulder, rose to her head. She jerked away, or would have jerked away, but his other hand came up to cup her jaw and hold her head still while his fingers explored her scalp. His touch was light, almost gentle, a sharp contrast to his face, his body, his voice—but she knew it didn't mean a thing. She had studied indigenous cultures in which the warriors treated their captives relatively gently until the moment of—

"Aah."

Sienna hissed in pain. The man grunted.

"You've got a lump behind your ear." His hands shifted, began a slow trip down her throat, along her shoulders.

"Don't," she said, but he paid no attention as he worked his way to her toes. His touch was efficient, not intimate, but that didn't keep it from adding to her terror.

"How many fingers?"

She blinked. "What?"

"How many fingers do you see?"

She looked at his upraised hand. "Three."

"And now?"

"Four. Who are you?"

Carefully, she rose on her elbows, felt the coldness of stone beneath her bare arms.

He leaned closer. She flinched back. He gave an impatient growl, caught hold of her shoulders and leaned toward her.

"What are you doing?"

"Checking your pupils."

It was unnerving. Those black eyes boring into hers.

"My pupils are fine."

"Turn your head. Again. Slowly. Good. I'm going to roll you over."

"You are *not* going to—"

But he did. His hands danced over her, his touch still impersonal. When he was finished, he turned her on her back, slid an arm under her shoulders and sat her up.

The world spun. There was a kind of buzzing sensation in her head, as if a swarm of tiny bees had found their way inside and set up housekeeping.

Sienna moaned.

The man's arm tightened around her. It was a strong, hard arm, deeply tanned by the sun, muscled and toned by work. She wanted to jerk away from him, but she didn't have the strength and even if she had, she knew he wouldn't have permitted it.

At last, the earth stopped spinning. She took a deep, shaky breath.

"I'm—I'm okay."

He let go of her. She swayed a little, and he cursed and wrapped his arm around her again.

"Put your head down."

"It isn't nec—"

"Put it down."

She complied. What choice was there when he was glaring at her? The last thing she wanted to do was anger a madman. He was angry enough already. At what? At her? Was anger a sign of psychosis? If only she'd paid more attention to those psych courses…

"Take another couple of deep breaths. That's it." He held

her a moment longer. Then he let go and put a few inches of distance between them. "Your name?"

It wasn't a question, it was a demand.

Should she tell him her name or shouldn't she? She'd once read that violent criminals generally didn't want to know anything about their victims, which was exactly why some shrinks thought you might save your life by making your kidnapper, your rapist, see you as an individual.

Your rapist, Sienna thought, and swallowed a wild rush of hysterical laughter. It sounded so mundane. Your hair stylist. Your bus driver.

Your rapist.

"Answer me. What's your name?"

She took a breath. "I'm Sienna Cummings. Who are you?"

"How did you get here?"

Where? She didn't realize she'd said the words aloud until his eyes narrowed to inky slits.

"Pleading amnesia won't work. Neither will avoiding my questions. How did you get here?"

She looked at him. "Where is here?" she said, in such a small voice that Jesse was tempted to believe her.

But she'd told him her name. Yeah, but that didn't mean anything. He'd dealt with enough wounded men to know that there was such a thing as selective memory loss. She might know her name but not anything else.

Or, he thought coldly, she might be lying through that soft-looking, rosy mouth.

"Here," he said grimly, "is my property."

"Blackwolf Canyon?" She shook her head. "You don't own this place."

"Trust me, lady. I damned well do. Every tree, every rock, every speck of dirt is mine."

"You don't own it," she repeated stubbornly.

Jesse almost laughed. She was damned sure of herself. Did she think she could plead ignorance and get away with what she'd planned?

He could categorize her easily enough. She was either a hippie who hadn't accepted the fact that the sixties were gone, or she was a thief.

There was a big market for relics from the long-gone past. "Sacred artifacts of Native Americans," the fat, easily frightened guy he'd caught on his land last year, despite the No Trespassing signs posted around his ten thousand acres, had called them, though real Native Americans simply referred to themselves as Indians.

As for the sacred part…

Complete, unadulterated crap.

Yeah, there were those of his people who were suckers for that kind of nonsense. He'd come close, as a boy, but Vietnam had sure as hell changed that. The stones, the glyphs, the pottery shards were nothing but stuff leftover from another time. The ledge didn't have any kind of woo-woo magical validity whatsoever.

But that didn't mean he'd let thieves and leftover flower children intrude upon it.

This place was his. He owned it, at least he'd own it until he signed the sale papers.

A quick appraisal told him this woman was no leftover flower child drawn to a romanticized version of the Old West. She wore no beads, no flowered gown, nor was her hair flowing. Instead her hair was pulled back from her face in a no-nonsense ponytail. She wore a plain cotton T-shirt and jeans that looked as if they'd seen a lot of use. She was a thief, plain and simple, and that she'd sneaked onto his property angered him almost as much as that he had not spotted her all the time he'd sat on his horse and stared at the mountain.

Yes, it had been dark as hell then, but so what? As a boy, as a soldier, he'd been trained to observe. To see things others didn't. And yet, she'd gotten past him.

Jesse's eyes narrowed. His skills were getting rusty. That would have to change. For now, though, he had to concentrate on how to get her off this ledge. Whatever she was, he didn't want her death on his conscience.

More to the point, he thought coldly, a corpse would bring not just the sheriff but a passel of reporters. More publicity was the last thing he wanted.

He shot a look to where the ledge jutted out over the floor of the canyon. The problem was getting her down without both of them ending up doing it the fast way. At the least, a fall would result in shattered bones. He needed rope, but he didn't have any, and riding forty minutes back to the house, leaving her here to the tender mercy of the sun and maybe the first curious check of the menu by an inquisitive buzzard, wasn't such a hot idea.

Rope, he thought. Not necessarily a lot of it, just enough to link her to him…

Quickly, he rose to his feet.

"Okay," he said brusquely. "Take off your belt."

Her face went white. "What?"

"Your belt." He was already unbuckling his. "Take it off."

"Don't do this." Her voice broke. "Please. Whoever you are, don't—"

His head came up. His eyes met hers and, hell, it all came together. The look on her face. The terror in her voice. She thought he was going to rape her. Why? Because he looked like what she undoubtedly thought of as a savage? Well, yeah.

Maybe. He was shirtless. He wore his hair long. There was an eagle talon half wrapped in rawhide hanging around his neck, a gift from his father.

To keep you safe, his father had said softly, the night before he had left for 'Nam.

The stripes on his cheeks were the only thing that had no reasonable explanation. Okay. Maybe they did. He'd come here to say goodbye to his land, his mountain, as a warrior. He'd spent less than a minute choosing between his army ODs and the paint of his people. He didn't believe in either, not anymore, but the link to those who'd preceded him could not be as easily discarded as a uniform, so he'd stripped off his shirt, striped his face, pulled his hair back with a strip of deerskin...

Jesse blew out a breath of exasperated comprehension.

The woman was a trespasser. She probably knew exactly where she was and that it was private land, but he couldn't fault her for leaping to the wrong conclusion at being told to take off her belt by a man who sure as hell didn't look like anything she was accustomed to.

"I need the belts to make a rope," he said.

"A rope?"

"To get us off this cliff."

She blinked. "To get us off this..."

He squatted beside her, grabbed her shoulders, forced her to turn her head and see the canyon. "Take a look, lady. We're on the side of a mountain. As if you didn't already know—"

"Oh God!" The words were a whisper, but they became louder and louder as she repeated them. "Oh God," she said, "oh God, oh God..."

She began to tremble. Tremble? The understatement of the year. She was shaking like an aspen leaf in a windstorm. Jesse shook her. Hard.

"Stop it!"

"I'm on the mountain. Blackwolf Mountain. In Blackwolf Canyon." She made a sound that might have been a laugh. "And this—this is the sacred stone!"

"Surprise, surprise," he said coldly.

She swung toward him, eyes wide, face still devoid of color.

"I was in the canyon. *In* it, do you understand? I was looking up at the mountain. At this ledge. At these stones and the sun and then—and then there was lightning and then I was here and no, it's impossible, impossible, impossible…."

If it was an act, it was a good one. Damn it, was she going into shock? No color. Sentences that made no sense.

He caught her wrist.

"Take it easy."

She laughed. It was the kind of laugh he'd heard wounded men make on the battlefield just before they gave it all up and went into shocked insanity. A knot formed in his belly. No. He was not going to let this woman go there. He had enough blood on his hands to last a lifetime.

"Take it easy," he said again. Her teeth were chattering, and he had nothing to warm her with except himself. On a low, angry curse, he wrapped his arms around her. "Calm down."

"D-did you h-hear what I said? I wa-was down there. At the bottom of this—this pile of rock. And then I wasn't. I wasn't d-down there, I was—I was here. And you—and you—"

"Come here," he growled, and he drew her hard against him. She struggled; he ignored it. After a few seconds, she gave a little sob; he felt the warmth of her breath against his naked flesh, the hot kiss of her tears. She felt delicate, almost fragile in his arms.

How on earth could she have had the strength to get up here? It didn't make sense.

Yes, she'd ignored his No Trespassing signs. She'd come here to steal artifacts. He was certain of that. But how had she climbed to this ledge? He knew how much muscle power it took, and he knew, too, that she didn't have it.

Not that her body was soft. Well, yes, it was. Soft, as only a woman could be soft. But she was fit. Toned. Her arms. Her belly, pressed to his.

Her breasts.

Rounded. Full. Ripe. And maybe he was the savage she thought him to be, after all, if he was in danger of turning hard while he held a woman he didn't know, and had every reason to dislike, in his arms.

Tonight, once he was off this damned mountain, Jesse thought grimly, he'd turn himself back into a man of the 1970s instead of the 1870s. He'd drive into town, hit the bar at Bozeman's best hotel and find himself a woman, a sweet-smelling, sexy East Coast tourist.

It was time to work off the past months of foolish celibacy. And if there was one thing that had never changed about him, it was that he'd never had trouble finding a beautiful woman to warm his bed.

After a couple of hours of that, he wouldn't get turned on holding a thief in his arms.

At least his thief had stopped shaking. She was making little hiccuping sounds. Carefully, he put her from him.

"Are you all right now?"

She nodded. Her hair had come loose. He'd thought it was brown, but it wasn't. It was gold. Beige. Brown. And what in hell did the color of her hair matter? Quickly, he got to his feet.

"Good," he said briskly. "Because you're going to have to listen closely. And cooperate, if we're going to get down safely."

She looked up at him. "What happened to me?"

Her voice was soft, still shocked. He couldn't afford that; she'd be too much a liability unless she got a grip on reality.

"Lightning."

She nodded. "I remember. It was green. How could lightning be green?"

It was an excellent question. Lightning, especially here, came in lots of colors. Red. White. A kind of electric blue. But green?

"Save the questions for later," he said brusquely. "Right now, what matters is getting off this ledge."

She swallowed. Ran the tip of her tongue over her dry lips. "I'm, uh, I'm not much for heights."

That explained why she hadn't tried to look into the canyon again. It sure as hell didn't explain how she'd gotten herself up here—and then a thought came to him.

"Do you have an accomplice?"

She stared up at him. "A what?"

"Is there anyone with you?" There had to be. Jesse moved to the edge of their stony platform and peered down, scanning the canyon floor as he'd once scanned for the 'Cong. Nobody. Nothing. Only Cloud, swishing his plume of a tail and munching on the leaves of a shrub.

"Yes," the woman said slowly. "Of course!" She stood up, keeping her eyes on the mountain, but she wobbled a little. Instinctively, Jesse moved quickly to her and gathered her against him. "Jack. Jack and the others."

"They abandoned you."

"No. They're at the foot of the mountain."

"They're gone," Jesse said harshly. "They let you risk your life for nothing. There's nothing here to steal. The guardian stones, the sacred stone itself, are too big. And there's nothing else." His mouth twisted. "Your people made off with whatever was up here fifty years ago."

"My people?" She glared up at him. "What's that supposed to mean?"

What, indeed? She was white. So what? He was, too. Half white, anyway, and what did it matter? He'd never given a damn about anyone's color. It was just that there was something about this woman that was disturbing.

"Okay," he said gruffly. "Here's the plan." An overstatement, but she didn't have to know that. "I'm going to link our belts together. I'll fasten one end around your wrist, the other around me. I'll go down first and you'll watch every move I make. You got that? Every single move, because one misstep and… Damn it, what now?"

Sienna Cummings was shaking her head. "I'm not climbing down this mountain."

"What will you do, then?" Jesse's voice dripped sarcasm. "Wish yourself down?"

The look she gave him was hot with defiance.

"I'm going to wake up."

Jesse raised his eyebrows. "Excuse me?"

"You heard me. I'm dreaming. This is a dream. It has to be. I am definitely not standing on a ledge halfway up a mountain, talking to a man who—who looks as if he stepped out of Central Casting for a movie starring John Wayne." A curl of golden brown hair blew over her lip; she shoved it behind her ear and her chin rose a little higher. "John Wayne is dead, and I am dreaming. End of story."

Jesse almost laughed. She was a tough piece of work. Whatever else she was, he had to admire her for that.

"I've got news for you, baby. John Wayne's alive. And this is no dream."

"Wrong on both counts," she said. If her chin went up any higher, she'd tumble over backward. "John Wayne is history.

And I am sound asleep in my tent. There's not a way in the world you can make me think otherwise." Her eyes—more violet than ever—narrowed. "This is not real."

"You're wasting valuable time. The sun's beating straight down. The descent's going to be tough enough without factoring in the heat."

"No," she said, though now there was a faint quaver in her voice, "I told you, this isn't real."

"It damned well is," Jesse snarled, and he proved it by pulling her into his arms, bending his head and covering her mouth with his.

CHAPTER THREE

SIENNA gasped as the stranger's arms closed around her.

"Don't," she said, or tried to say, but he was too quick, too strong, too determined. She tried to twist her face away but that didn't work, either. All he had to do was slide one hand into her hair, cup the back of her head and bring his mouth down on hers.

There was no way to call this a kiss. It was a hard imprint of his flesh on hers, a ruthless demonstration of sheer masculine power.

He wanted to show her that she was helpless against him.

But she wasn't.

Her work took her to places that were often desolate and dangerous. She'd studied martial arts, and her instructor's advice— *look for an opening or create one*—had saved her on a dig in the jungles of Peru, as well as on the streets of Manhattan. It would save her now. All she had to do was force herself to relax. Her assailant would follow suit by easing his hold on her. Then she'd bring up her knee and jam it, hard, into his crotch.

Wrong. Nothing about him relaxed.

If anything, as soon as she stopped struggling, he drew her even closer.

Her palms spread helplessly over sun-heated skin stretched taut over hard-muscled flesh. He tilted her head back, giving him greater access to her mouth. Sienna whimpered and tried to bite him. It was another misjudgment. As soon as her lips parted, his tongue swept into her mouth.

And everything changed.

What had been cold calculation turned hot and wild. She felt the press of his erection against her belly; the taste of him on her lips became dark and exciting. She heard herself make a little sound, almost a purr. *No,* she thought desperately, but even as she thought it, she was leaning into him, rising to him….

With a suddenness that left her reeling, he caught her by the shoulders and put her from him. She knew her cheeks were flushed, but when she looked at him, his face was expressionless. That frightened her even more than the way he'd kissed her…and the way she'd reacted.

Except, she hadn't. She hadn't! She wasn't the kind of woman turned on by displays of macho male power. She was a woman of the twenty-first century and behavior like this had gone out decades ago.

Still, for that one, heart-stopping instant…

Sienna forced the thought aside. She looked up at the stranger. Deliberately, slowly, she wiped the back of her hand over her lips and then against her jeans.

"Do that again," she said in a low voice, "and I'll kill you."

"Give me a hard time again," he said in mocking imitation of her, "I'll leave you up here and the only life you'll take will be your own." His mouth twisted. "Do you get it now? This is reality. You're not dreaming."

"Is using force the way you generally make a point?"

Something flickered in his eyes. "Only when there's no other choice. A man does what he has to do."

"So does a woman." Her chin came up. "You might keep that in mind."

"Hang on to that attitude. It might just help save you."

From him? From the climb down? Sienna wasn't foolish enough to ask. This was not a man to push too far, at least not until she was safely back in civilization with Jack and the others. For now, doing what she had to do made sense, and what she had to do was get off this ledge.

"The belt," he said, holding out his hand.

He'd already stripped his from the loops of his jeans. She hesitated, then undid hers and gave it to him.

He worked quickly, his big hands moving with surprising grace as he joined the two lengths of leather. When he finished, he tugged hard at both ends. The leather held, but so what? Belts weren't made to support the weight of two people descending a mountain. His improvised rope wasn't long enough or strong enough or—

Thunder rumbled from somewhere behind the mountain. She looked up. Dark clouds were moving in. The sky looked ominous. Nerves made her sweep the tip of her tongue over her lips....

And she tasted him.

Anger. Power. Determination. And the darker tastes of man and desire.

"Ready?"

She blinked. The man was wrapping one end of the joined belts around his wrist. It was a big wrist but it matched the rest of him. His height. His shoulders. His powerful arms, ridged abdomen, long legs...

"Keep looking at me like that," he said in a low voice, "you're asking for trouble."

A flush rose in Sienna's face. "What's your name?"

He looked at her as if she were crazy. Maybe she was, but before she stepped into space, real or imagined, it seemed she should at least know who he was.

"Does it matter?"

She turned, shot a glance at the yawning distance between them and the canyon floor. Then she looked at him.

"Yes," she said stubbornly. "It does."

Just when she thought he wasn't going to answer, he shrugged those big shoulders.

"It's Jesse."

Sienna stared at him. "Jesse?"

"Jesse Blackwolf."

"But—but—"

"You wanted my name. You've got it. Now, let's get moving before that storm hits."

"But..." she said again, and he grabbed her wrist.

"No more talking. You got that?"

She got it, all right. Besides, what could she say? How could she possibly tell him that he could not, absolutely could not be who he said he was, that Jesse Blackwolf, if he'd turned up, was in his sixties? So she kept quiet as he wrapped a section of the belt around her wrist, secured it, then gave it a tug that seemed to meet with his satisfaction.

"Do everything I do," he said. "Concentrate on—" He grabbed her by the shoulders, hoisted her to her toes. "Listen to me, if you want to survive. The rules are simple."

"Rules?" she said, with a nervous laugh.

"Rules. Five of them. Do not look down. Do not look up. Keep your eyes on your hands and feet and on me. Pay attention to what I say. Obey what I say, without question. Understand?"

She didn't have enough saliva in her mouth to answer. Instead, she nodded her head, but the truth was, the only thing she actually understood was that she'd never been so scared in her life.

He turned his back to her and took a step forward.

"Wait!"

He looked over his shoulder, face taut with impatience.

"What now?"

"How—I mean, what, exactly, am I supposed to do?"

"I just told you."

"No. I mean—I mean, I've seen people climb rocks. Should I search for handholds? Dig my toes into the crevices? Stay in one place until I've found the next—"

"Are you deaf, woman? You do what I do. Nothing else. And stop trying to analyze everything. This is a mountain. The ground is forty feet down. There's a score of places in between where we can break our necks." His eyes narrowed. "You're just going to have to trust me."

Trust him? A man who couldn't possibly exist, standing with her on a mountain she couldn't possibly have climbed? A man who snapped orders like a general but looked like a savage and thought that the way to handle a woman who asked questions and proved she had a brain was to kiss her into submission?

"You have no other choice."

It was as if he'd heard what she was thinking.

And he was right. What could she do but step off into space behind him? Maybe she *was* dreaming. Or hallucinating. Or whatever you did when you were unconscious. Maybe, indeed, but she was stuck up here, anyway, with no way down except this.

A whimper inched its way into her throat. She tried to stop it. Too late. Jesse Blackwolf, the man who called himself Jesse Blackwolf, had obviously heard it.

"Scared?"

What was the logic in lying? Still, she wasn't going to sound pathetic about it.

"Damned right, I'm scared!"

He smiled. It didn't last more than a second; it was the barely perceptible lift of one corner of his mouth, but it was a smile and it changed him from terrifying male to gorgeous man—and was she crazy, noticing such a thing at a moment like this?

"Good," he said. "You'd have to be a fool not to be scared, and a fool's the last person I'd want tied to me right now." He reached out, one big hand cupping her chin. "Obey me. Be a good girl and I promise, I'll get you down safely."

Obey him. Be a good girl. Even now, with the coppery taste of fear on her tongue, Sienna almost laughed. Nobody had said anything remotely like that to her since she was twelve, but this didn't seem the time or place to correct him on what her Women's Studies prof called gender issues that still existed more than thirty years after the women's lib movement.

"Is it a deal?"

She nodded. He leaned forward and brushed his mouth lightly over hers.

"For luck," he said.

And then he turned his back to her and stepped off the ledge.

At least, that was the way it looked.

He hadn't stepped off it, though. His head and shoulders appeared as if from nowhere, along with an extended hand.

"Let's go," he said briskly.

"I'm coming," Sienna said. And she would—in a decade or two. Right now, her feet seemed glued to the sacred stone.

"Remember what I said? Just do what I tell you to do."

"Something you should know about me," she said with

forced lightness as she inched forward. "I never do what any-one tells me to do. Especially a man."

"You want to burn bras, do it somewhere else."

Okay. This time, frightened as she was, she did laugh at the old-fashioned phrase.

"Good. Relax. Take a deep breath. Another. And give me your hand."

"In a minute."

"Now," he commanded. "Hear that thunder? The storm's getting closer. Bad weather's not a pleasant thing to experi-ence on an exposed ledge."

A convincing roar of thunder followed his words.

"Sienna! Give me your hand."

Who could possibly argue with such authority?

Not me, Sienna thought, and she took Jesse's hand and stepped off the cliff.

A gentle rain had started by the time they reached the can-yon floor.

As for the climb down… She had no clear memory of it. Halfway down, scree coming loose under her feet, fingernails torn off by desperately digging into cracks that only a very generous person would call handholds, she'd finally taken Jesse's best advice.

She'd stopped thinking.

It had been easier after that, but he'd still twice saved her from plummeting to earth.

Each misstep had left her hanging, one hand clutching the rocky face of the mountain while her feet dangled in midair. Each time, he'd clasped his fingers tightly around her wrist, his face contorting with determination as he steadied her until she found a foothold.

Now they were down. And this time, when the man who said he was Jesse Blackwolf said "good girl" as she tumbled into his waiting arms, she didn't give a damn for gender issues.

She was simply happy to be alive.

"Th-thank you," she said in a shaky whisper.

It was all she could manage, but it was enough.

Jesse nodded, held her in the circle of his arms and wondered if he ought to tell her she'd surprised him with her courage.

No. Not now. There was no point to it. Why compliment her for creating a situation in which she'd risked both their lives? Besides, they had to get out of here before the storm hit with full force. It was going to be a bad one; the signs were all there. The dark sky, the wind, the thunder and lightning…

This would be a storm that would turn the lazy creek that ran between the canyon and his ranch into a raging torrent.

So, any second now, he'd let go of the woman in his arms.

But not just yet.

She needed to share his body warmth. Her teeth were chattering; her skin was icy. She might be going into shock. Anything was possible in the aftermath of danger.

He'd seen men—trained warriors—face the worst kind of imminent death and survive, then all but collapse when the danger was over.

Sienna Cummings had just come through that type of situation.

He'd made it sound as if getting down the mountain required nothing but her compliance. He knew better. The descent had called for guts and determination. She'd shown both.

Of course, she'd gotten up the mountain in the first place and that was almost as difficult. How had she done it? That was still the $64,000 question.

Damned if he could come up with an answer.

Maybe somebody had helped her. Climbed with her. That guy she'd mentioned. Jim or John. Jack. Yeah. Jack. Had he gone up with her? And then, what, left her?

What kind of man would abandon a woman that way?

Endless questions. No answers. None he could answer right now, at any rate, not with the storm almost on them and Sienna still trembling in his arms.

He could feel the race of her heart. Feel the soft whisper of her breath against his skin. He gathered her even closer, leaned his chin on the top of her head. Her hair was soft; it smelled of rain and, very faintly, of lilacs.

"Easy," he said. "We're down. You're okay."

He wasn't sure she'd heard him. Then she drew a shuddering breath.

"I didn't think we'd make it."

"Blackwolf Mountain and I have known each other a very long time."

She gave a little laugh. "A good thing."

Not really, he thought, but she had no need to know that.

"You all right now?"

"I'm fine."

She wasn't. She was still shaking, her face devoid of color. And she was a mess.

Her hair was a mass of curls. He'd already seen the bump on her head. She'd broken her fingernails. Her jeans were torn and so was her T-shirt. Sweat and now the steadily increasing rain had plastered them to her, outlining her body. It was delicate but as lush and feminine as a man could want.

He could feel her belly and her thighs against his. Could feel her breasts pressed against his chest, the pebbled nipples seeming to burn against his naked flesh. The pebbling told him she was chilled. And braless. And that her breasts were gently uptilted as if in readiness for a man's mouth.

He shut his eyes, willing the all-too-vivid image away, deliberately replacing it with an image of her face. That was safer.

She had a pretty face, but more than that, an intelligent one. Bottom line, she looked nothing like a thief or a flower child still caught up by the nonsense of the prior decade.

What she looked like was a woman a man would want in his bed. Not a man like him. His secrets were too dark; the shadows that engulfed him too ugly. But, yes, some man would want a woman like this.

He felt himself stir against her. He pulled back, hoping she hadn't felt his erection. *Goddamn it,* he thought coldly. What in hell was this?

He had, absolutely, been without a woman far too long. There was no other reason Sienna Cummings would turn him on. Besides, the facts were simple. She had invaded his land, climbed his mountain.

All he wanted was to send her on her way.

"Okay," he said gruffly, dropping his arms to his sides, "let's get mov—"

A roar of thunder drowned him out. Lightning sizzled across the sky. White lightning. And as if someone had hit a switch, the dark clouds opened up, spewing torrential rain. Instantly, they were soaked from head to foot. His intruder gave a little shriek and raised her hands as if to shelter under them. The gesture was useless, but he couldn't blame her. The temperature had dropped at least twenty degrees and the rain was ice cold and as sharp as needles.

Jesse grabbed her arm. She broke free, swung in a circle.

"What are you doing?" he yelled. It was the only way to make himself heard over the rain.

"Looking for my people."

"I told you, your boyfriend abandoned you."

"No. That's impossible!"

"Listen, lady, you want to argue, argue with yourself. I'm going to head for shelter."

She looked at him. He wanted to laugh. The last creature he'd ever seen this wet and woebegone had been a calf that had wandered into a stream.

"You coming with me or not?"

She gave a dejected nod. He put two fingers in his mouth and whistled. The piercing sound carried over the roar of the rain and Cloud came thundering toward them. Sienna shrieked and jumped behind Jesse. That did it; the laughter he'd choked back a moment ago erupted in a snort.

"It's a horse," he said. "Not a mountain lion."

"Don't you have a truck?"

She was impossible. Jesse mounted the stallion, reached down and held his out his hand.

"You want transportation, this is it. You coming with me? Yes or no?"

She stared up at him. Then she clasped his hand and hoisted herself onto the animal's back. A good thing, too. The last thing he'd have wanted to do was wrestle a wet, unwilling woman onto the saddleless back of an equally wet horse.

"Hold on."

Sienna blinked. Hold on? To what? There was no saddle, there was nothing but man and horse.

"Put your arms around me. That's it. Tighter, unless you want to make this ride hanging on to Cloud's tail."

He was right. Besides, a few minutes ago, his arms had been around her. Stupid to hesitate now, she thought, and wrapped her arms around his waist.

His skin was smooth and wet and warm. She felt the taut muscles of his belly contract under her fingers. It made her breath catch and she started to pull back, but at just that moment, he dug his heels into the animal's flanks and the horse surged forward as if he were going to leap into the air and fly.

Sienna gave a muffled shriek and tightened her grip on Jesse until her breasts and belly were pressed tightly against his back.

"Good girl," he shouted.

Sienna rolled her eyes. Another metaphorical sexist pat on the head, but what could she do about it? And, really, what did it matter?

If this was all happening, she'd be free of this man as soon as they reached, well, wherever they were heading. Bozeman, she hoped. Jack was probably there, waiting for her with the others, and surely he'd have some rational explanation for everything.

If this wasn't happening, if she was dreaming, she'd wake up.

Those were the only two possibilities, and neither involved dealing with Jesse Blackwolf for more than just another little while.

Those *were* the only two possibilities…weren't they?

No, she thought uneasily, they weren't.

What if that green lightning had struck her? What if she was in a coma? What if she were lying comatose in a hospital bed, having wildly exotic dreams or whatever you called the stuff that filled your head while your brain was on medical hiatus?

It made sense that she might dream of a place she'd spent months and months studying. And, okay, it even made sense that she might dream of being rescued by a dark and dangerous man. Her life centered around her studies, but she was still a woman. And she was a scholar of ancient civilizations.

She'd never been the type for romantic fantasies, but if she were…

If she were, this man would fit the bill.

A coma made absolute sense.

And, actually, it was the far better choice, because otherwise, she was back to square one. How had she ended up on that ledge? Where was Jack? What was she doing, racing through a flooding canyon with a man who looked like an Indian warrior?

Sienna jammed her eyes closed. A coma, for sure. Any minute now, she'd wake up, see that she was in a hospital room….

"Hang on tight," Jesse said.

Her eyes snapped open. What looked like the ocean was dead ahead, a rushing torrent of water that they surely could not ford. But the stallion plunged into the swollen stream without hesitation.

Could you drown in a stream you'd created in your mind?

God, she was going crazy!

Water coursed over her feet, her calves, her thighs. The horse couldn't keep his footing, not in this, but he did, he did as Jesse urged him on.

"Good boy," he said, and Sienna laughed and laughed and she knew, she *knew* there was a note of hysteria in her voice, but she couldn't help it. All she could do was clutch the man who was not real despite what he'd said, press her cheek to his strong, hard, not-real-either back, and wait for the moment this would end.

An eternity later, the horse slowed to a walk.

"We're here," Jesse said.

Sienna sat up straight. They'd stopped moving, but the world was a blur of heavily falling rain. Good. She wasn't ready to see past it. Not just yet.

"Where?"

He threw a long leg over the stallion's head and dismounted. His big hands closed around her waist; he lifted her from the horse to the ground and she sent up a silent, tiny prayer of hope.

Maybe she was coming out of the coma. Maybe she'd see the comforting white walls of a hospital room.

Or maybe not. Maybe she was still trapped in a place that didn't exist, and when she opened her eyes, she'd see, what? A log cabin? A tepee? A corral full of piebald ponies?

She took a deep breath. And forced herself to look. At the torrent of rain falling from a leaden sky…

And at all the rest.

There was no hospital room. No tepee. No log cabin. Well, not unless you called a sprawling, magnificent structure of cypress and glass, acres of glass, a cabin. There was also a corral. A huge barn. And a side yard.

Not a dream. Not a dream. Not a dream.

And not a coma. It couldn't be. She didn't know enough about cars and trucks to have populated the side yard with a bright red car so long and low she knew it had to be foreign, a black pickup truck and what she figured was a battered Jeep.

Each vehicle bore a license plate. Each read "Montana." And each read—each read…

Sienna's heart leaped into her throat. She swung toward Jesse.

"The date," she whispered. "What's the date?"

He stared at her. Maybe he hadn't understood her. She knew her voice sounded choked. She cleared her throat, not certain she could form the words again. But she didn't have to.

His eyes narrowed. "What now?" he said coldly. "Is this another part of the game?"

"No game. Just tell me, please. What's the date?"

"June 22, as you well know."

"Not June 21? The solstice…"

"It fell on the twenty-second this year. That only happens—"

She could almost feel the blood draining from her head. "It only happens every four hundred years. I know that."

"So?"

"So…" She licked her lips. There was only one last question to ask, but she was afraid to ask it. "So the last time it happened the year was—the year was 1975."

Jesse put his fists on his hips. Legs apart, eyes locked to hers, he looked less savage but twice as dangerous.

"*Was* 1975? Give me a break, okay? This *is* 1975."

"Now?" Sienna said calmly. "Right now, it's—"

Her eyes rolled up into her head and she crumpled to the ground.

CHAPTER FOUR

ONE second, Sienna Cummings was looking at him as if one of them was crazy.

The next, her eyes rolled up and she fell to the ground. Or she would have, if Jesse hadn't caught her. She was limp, her face bloodless, her lashes dark crescents against high cheekbones.

Great, he thought, clasping her shoulders as he held her up. A trespasser who'd perfected the art of Victorian swoons.

If she thought that was going to change anything, she was wrong.

"Miss Cummings," he said roughly. "Come on. Open your eyes."

He shook her, not altogether gently. Nothing happened, not even a flutter of those long, dark lashes. His mouth thinned. She really had fainted, right in the middle of what they'd have labeled a typhoon on the other side of the world.

And he was stuck with her.

The stallion nuzzled his shoulder.

"Yeah, okay," Jesse said grimly. He wrapped one arm around the woman, slipped the bridle from Cloud's massive head and ran a rough hand over the animal's neck. "Go home, boy." The big horse trotted for the open barn door and Jesse clamped both arms around his unwelcome guest and did the same, running for the shelter of the house.

Her head fell back; the heavy rain beat down on her up-turned face and he cursed softly, cupped her head and brought her face to his shoulder.

Thunder snarled; lightning sliced through the sky, sizzling like cold water hitting a hot griddle.

No question, it was going to be a long day.

He took the wide steps to the porch fast, shifted the woman's weight to free a hand so he could throw open the massive oak door. Not that there was all that much weight to shift. She was a skinny thing. Okay. Not skinny. The rain, his check of her earlier, the way she'd fit into his arms, had made it obvious she had all the requisite soft, curving parts.

As if that mattered a damn.

He stepped quickly inside the oak-floored foyer, kicked the door shut behind him. The sound of the rain lessened, but the thunder growled like a wild beast seeking its prey.

He went straight for the living room. His unwelcome guest was still out. And now she was trembling. No surprise there. The rain had soaked her to the bone. He had to warm her before hypothermia set in.

There was a stack of newspapers on the long white sofa. He swept them to the floor and put her down on the sofa, grabbed the old patchwork quilt that hung over the sofa's back and covered her with it.

"Hey," he said. "Cummings. Open your eyes."

She gave a low moan. Well, that was a start.

"Come on," he said sharply. "Look at me."

A faint flutter of her lashes. That was all. Damn it, he thought furiously. Why couldn't she have climbed somebody else's pile of rocks? Gone after some other supposedly sacred ledge? The pictographs, the legend of the Blackwolf stones, were hardly the only ones out there.

She moaned again. Turned her head from side to side. Whispered something. He bent closer, tried to make it out. *No,* maybe?

"No, what?" he said.

She didn't answer. She was still out. And, hell, she looked as fragile as his mother's bone china dinnerware.

A muscle knotted in his jaw.

Where was the tough, don't-screw-with-me babe who'd faced him on the ledge? He didn't want her fragile, didn't want her helpless. He didn't want to be responsible for her.

He didn't want to be responsible for anyone, ever again.

If only he hadn't given in to that stupid desire to ride to the canyon and see the solstice one final time. If only he'd stayed here, right here, because what in hell did the canyon or the solstice or any of it matter? If only. If only…

"Stop it," he said out loud.

A man did what he had to do. Life's great lesson, he thought bitterly, even if you were dealing with a trespasser, a thief…

Or a woman.

This one, at least, would be gone by tomorrow.

Jesse stood straight, headed quickly for the kitchen, grabbed a towel from the rack next to the sink and dried his naked arms and chest. He was chilled, too, his jeans soggy with rainwater, but first things first. Deal with the woman. Get her out of those wet clothes, dry her, get her conscious enough to drink something hot and sweet. The idea was to elevate her core temp, keep it from sliding to the danger point.

And call the doctor.

By the time he arrived, the woman would be okay, but the doc could check her over, just to play it safe. And he could take her back to town with him. To a motel. To the hospital. Who cared where he took her?

He grabbed the phone, started to dial the number—and realized the thing was dead.

"Damn it!"

Of course the miserable hunk of plastic was dead. Heavy rain, lightning, high winds, for all he knew a grizzly rubbing its ass against one of the telephone poles was more than enough to take down the phone lines. It happened with regularity.

Besides, what good would a call have done? The doc couldn't make it out this far any more than he could do the trip in reverse. Trees would be down, roads buried under sheets of water. The creek that ran between the ranch and the highway would make the stream they'd crossed heading out of the canyon look like a puddle.

There was an emergency chopper in Bozeman but it couldn't fly in this stuff.

"Okay," he muttered.

Forget the medical help. A man did what he had to do, he thought again, and he got started. It was a short list, but a vital one.

He turned up the thermostat as high as it would go. The burner kicked in with a throaty roar. Start a fire in the fireplace. Fire sucked warm air out of a room, but with the Cummings woman lying where she was, she'd get the best of the heat coming up through the registers and from the hearth.

Now he needed towels. And blankets. Tea. Honey. A kettle of boiling water.

Keeping busy was good. He felt purposeful, less aware of the woman as an unwanted intrusion and more as a problem to deal with. He'd always been good at handling problems.

Handling people was different.

Linda had thrown that at him, toward the end, and he hadn't even tried to refute it.

He checked the woman again, then went swiftly through the house, collecting a bunch of oversized bath sheets, an armload of blankets. A fast stop in the kitchen to put the water on to boil.

Back to Sienna Cummings.

Already, simply from being indoors, wrapped in the quilt, heat coming up and the fire going, she looked a little better. More color in her face. Less labored breathing. She was still shivering, though. Not a good sign. He knew it could indicate that her temperature was not just low but still dropping.

He had to warm her, and fast.

"Miss Cummings. Can you hear me?" He squatted beside the couch, took her wrist, checked her pulse. A little thready but nothing too bad. "Come on," he said briskly. "Open your eyes." He leaned closer, spoke louder. "Look at me," he ordered.

And she did.

Her eyes opened. Her gaze met his…and slid right on by.

He cupped her chin, spoke her name sharply, gave that up and went for a light slap across her face.

Still nothing. Time to move on to step two.

"I'm going to undress you," he told her. "Get you out of those wet clothes. Okay?"

She murmured something he couldn't understand. It didn't matter. If he left her like this, wet and chilled, she'd die.

Working quickly, he looped an arm around her shoulders. Sat her up. Her head fell forward; her face tucked itself against his throat, just as when he'd found her on the mountain. Her breath was soft and warm; the whisper of it sent a shudder of awareness through him.

Just a natural reaction, he told himself, what happened when air fanned over your skin.

He slipped his hand under the back of her T-shirt, pushed the wet fabric up as far as it would go. Her skin was cold, almost icy, against his palm.

It was not a good sign.

He should have gotten her into dry clothes right away instead of wasting precious minutes thinking about not wanting this kind of responsibility.

Quickly but carefully, he shifted her in his arms, sat her up, held her there when she started to slip back against the couch cushions. He worked the T-shirt up over her belly. The skin there was slightly warmer: that was good. The natural instinct of a healthy body was to keep vital organs warm.

The skin there was smooth, too. The fact registered somewhere in the back of his mind. It had nothing to do with getting her out of the wet shirt, but he was aware of it. Just part of his head taking inventory of her condition, he told himself briskly, as he dragged the drenched cotton up and over her breasts.

Getting her arms out of the sleeves wasn't easy, but at last he tugged the shirt over her head and tossed it aside.

And, damn, she was beautiful.

No bra, which he'd already figured. Uptilted nipples, which he'd figured, as well. But not their color. Delicate. Pale. An innocent pink.

A lie. Nothing about her was innocent.

Jesse knotted his jaw, dragged his eyes from her breasts to her jeans. Getting them off would be a walk in the park compared to getting her out of that shirt.

Wrong.

The jeans closed with two small buttons above the fly. The buttons were tough to open because the denim was so wet, but he finally got them through the buttonholes and undid the zipper.

She made a little sound. A murmur. He looked at her face just in time to see her eyelids flicker.

"Miss Cummings? Can you hear me?"

No answer. Okay. Time to finish undressing her. He didn't know why it was bothering him so much but it was. He'd been trained in first aid. She was probably a victim of hypothermia. He wasn't a man. She wasn't a woman.

But when he slipped his hands under her bottom and lifted her hips toward him, a picture flashed through his mind. Him, doing this same thing. Lifting her to him. To strip away her jeans, yes...

As part of making love to her.

His hands stilled.

He could see it all. Her face, flushed with pleasure. Her eyes, opened and hot on his. Her lips forming his name, her arms reaching for him, the jeans coming down, down, down her long legs and revealing...

White cotton underpants.

That was what they revealed. White cotton, as innocent-looking as the sweet pink of her nipples.

God, she was beautiful. Her femininity. Her face. Her hair, a mass of gold-streaked curls. And he, he was...

A groan broke from his throat. He was a no-good SOB, was what he was. What kind of man got a hard-on when he was dealing with an unconscious woman?

Quickly, he laid her back against the cushions. Dumped the now-wet quilt, grabbed another blanket and wrapped it around her. Yeah, but the sofa was damp. No good. He lifted her in his arms and carried her to his bedroom. There were four other bedrooms in the house, but he hadn't furnished any of them beyond the basics, not after Linda left.

What was the point?

He lived alone.

No woman. No friends. No guests. He preferred it that way.

His bed was big, covered with a simple black duvet. He folded it back, put the woman beneath it and drew it to her chin. She was starting to stir, her color was back.

Good.

Okay. He'd get her a heating pad. A big mug of tea. But first, he'd take care of himself, if only for long enough to get out of his soaked jeans and put on sweats. He'd stayed active, he wasn't a likely candidate for hypothermia, but he wouldn't do his uninvited guest much good if he got sick.

Working fast, he pulled the rawhide from his hair and rubbed a towel over his face, obliterating the stripes of black paint. The eagle talon danced against his chest as he tugged off his wet jeans, then his boxers. He yanked open a drawer, found sweats, stepped into the bottoms, pulled them up—

Sienna Cumming's eyes shot open. Jesse breathed a sigh of relief.

"Good," he said gruffly. "You're conscious."

Her eyes were blurry. Her tongue slicked over her lips.

"Who…? Where…?"

Confusion was common in cases of hypothermia. You lived in these mountains, you made it a point to know these things.

Jesse sat down next to her, tried to look reassuring.

"You're fine," he said briskly. "You, ah, you passed out. The rain—"

She turned her head. Looked around her, then looked again at him.

"Blackwolf Mountain," she said thickly. "The sacred stone—"

"Right."

"The lightning."

"Yes."

"Rain," she said. "And cold. So cold…"

A shudder went through her. Enough conversation. She wasn't warm enough yet.

"Look," Jesse started to say, "we can discuss this when—"

The kettle shrieked. She jumped like a doe taken down by a hunter's bow.

"It's the kettle, that's all. I'll make some tea. We can talk then. Okay?"

She didn't answer. Her gaze was moving over him. He hadn't had a shirt on when she'd first seen him and he didn't have one on now, but it felt different, maybe because he knew she was almost naked beneath the duvet.

Maybe because she knew it, too.

Something was happening behind those violet eyes. It was like watching her watching a movie. Emotions swept over her face. Awareness. Fear. Terror.

"Ohmygod," she said, "ohmygod…"

Enough. This was where he'd come in.

"Take it easy," he said, his voice rough. "Just take it—"

The lights went out.

Just like that. Out. No blinking. No going off, coming on, then going off. One second, the lights were on. They next, the room went dark.

Dark? It was black as pitch.

That figured. It was midafternoon. They'd lost hours between getting down the mountain and the wild ride home, plus the raging storm had obliterated whatever had remained of daylight.

Hell.

He should have figured on the lights going out. The electric lines up this high were only marginally more reliable than the ones for the telephone.

Idiot that he was, the one thing he hadn't installed when he built the house was a generator. He had one on order but it was a big job—it had to be specially built and it wouldn't be ready for another few months.

Jesse blinked, waited for his eyes to acclimate to the darkness. His other senses had already gone on full alert. He could smell Sienna's skin, that delicate lilac scent he'd noticed hours ago. And he could hear her teeth chattering.

Was she shaking again?

He reached out. Felt for her...

"Get away from me!"

"Listen, lady—"

He heard her scramble up against the pillows. She was breathing hard; the sound was raw. Just what he needed. Instant replay of what had happened an hour ago, right before she passed out.

"You're using up energy," he said coldly.

She didn't answer.

Jesse stood, put his hands on his hips. Took a long breath. He had candles. A Coleman lantern. A Coleman stove. He also had a crazy woman on his hands, but maybe some light and hot food would bring her to her senses.

"Stay where you are," he said brusquely. "I'll be right back."

It took him a few minutes to get the gas lantern and stove from where he stored his hunting and camping gear. Matches were easy; he grabbed a handful from a drawer in the kitchen. Got a fat candle from a cupboard and lit it.

"Okay," he said, trying to sound cheerful as he used its wavering light to guide him back to the bedroom. "We're all set—"

She was gone.

Gone? How? Where? Jesse turned on his heel, made a

complete circle, the candle held out in front of him as he checked the big room. Maybe the woman wasn't the only one who was crazy. Maybe he'd imagined her. Linda had all but accused him of being nuts.

What happened to you? she'd said. *You're a different man since you came back, Jesse. I'm afraid of you.*

But no, he wasn't crazy. His trespasser had been lying right there. The duvet was flung aside, the top sheet was missing, a strand of golden hair was on the black pillowcase.

Thunder shook the house.

"Miss Cummings?" Stupid. She was naked. He'd undressed her. What was the point of formalities? "Sienna? Sienna, where are you?"

Silence. He went to the door, checked the hall. There wasn't a sign of her.

Another roar of thunder. Another flash of lightning. And there they were. Footprints, small, highly arched. A woman's delicate prints, leading to his dressing room…

That was where he found her. At the far end of the oversized space, her back to the wall, the top sheet clutched to her chin.

"Sienna," he said sharply, "what the hell do you think you're doing?"

"I can tell you what I'm *not* doing," she said. "I am not letting you rape me."

"Are we back to that? I have no intention of—"

"Get out of my way."

"Sienna. Listen to me. You're not making any sense. You're not thinking straight."

"I am. I am thinking very, very straight."

"You're trembling. Do you have any idea how dangerous—"

"How dangerous you are." Her chin came up. Or it would

have, if she wasn't having so much difficulty not sinking to the floor. "Yes. I do."

"Damn it, woman! It's not me that's dangerous!"

"Yes, you are. And I'm not going to sta-stand here and—and—"

But she wasn't standing. She was sliding down the wall. Jesse got to her just in time—and took a weak but well-placed fist to the jaw by way of thanks. He grabbed her hands in one of his as he lifted her into his arms.

"Stop it!"

Her hands flailed at his face. Her sharp teeth sank into his biceps and he growled a warning, shifted position, hoisted her over his shoulder, sheet and all, and strode into the bedroom.

Now what?

Getting some light in here would change things, but only an octopus could hang on to a struggling female and turn on a lantern at the same time. If he put her down, she'd run again. Or grab something and slug him with it.

"Hold still," he ordered. "Hold still or so help me, I'll get a rope—a real rope—and tie you up."

That did it. She went limp. He waited, counted silently to ten. Then he eased her off his shoulder, set her on her feet but kept her balled fists clasped in his hand.

"I want to talk. Just talk. You got that?"

She made a sound. A snort of derision. Another good sign. Some of that toughness was coming back.

"I have no interest in you sexually." Okay, a lie, but a meaningless one. His hormones were interested but he certainly wasn't. That made it easy to keep his tone cold. Almost clinical. "You're not my type. And just so we get this straight…" His lips twitched. "I don't generally have to force women into my bed. Got it?"

An endless silence. Then she nodded.

"Great." Carefully, he let go of her hands. "Can we talk now?"

She swallowed dryly. Her face was turning pink.

"I'm—I'm naked."

Her voice was low. He felt a twinge of sympathy—and a twinge of that damned hormonal lust. It made his response harsh.

"Next time I'm stuck with a woman who looks like a half-drowned cat, I'll pass on trying to save her ass. Anything else?"

"I don't know where I am."

"My place. Blackwolf Ranch. I brought you here, remember?"

"That isn't what I meant," she said quickly. "I meant—I meant—"

She fell silent. Too late. He knew what she meant. That nonsense about the year. She didn't know it, or she couldn't remember it. Something like that.

That she was so completely confused mystified him. It had to be the after-effects of the lightning strike. He had a set of Grolier's; he'd look it up in the encyclopedia once the power came back on. Reassure her. Reassure himself that she wasn't—

"I'm fine now."

His eyebrows rose. "Yeah?"

"Everything just, you know, clicked into place. It was the, uh, the cold. The rain. Shock. That can cause confusion. Right?"

Her lips curved into a smile. It was about as phony as anything he'd ever seen, but he decided to pretend he'd bought into it. It would make her easier to deal with.

"Good. I'm glad to hear it."

"So, if you'd just give me something to wear—"

"I'll get you something of mine. Sweats. They'll swim on you but—"

"That'll be fine." She inhaled, let the breath out on a long whoosh. "And thank you. For all you've done."

Her smile was real this time. He felt its impact, the softness of her voice, sink into him like a caress. Something twisted in his belly; it was a feeling he'd all but forgotten, a sense of connection that he'd thought he'd never feel again. He didn't like it, didn't need it, and the sooner she understood that, the better.

"I only did what I had to do," he said coldly. Her smile died and he turned away from her, grabbed the Coleman lamp and lit it. Half the room filled with its welcome light.

"Okay," he said briskly. "I'll get the sweats. Once you're dressed, head down the hall to the kitchen… What now?"

Her mouth was trembling. Her eyes glittered. She shook her head; her hair fell around her face, obscuring it.

"Nothing," she whispered—but she was a lousy liar.

Of course it was something. His coldness? Her confusion? Whatever it was, she was weeping. Soundlessly, but weeping just the same.

Don't be a fool, Blackwolf, Jesse told himself. *Just keep walking.*

He wanted to. He started to. But halfway to the door, she said "Jesse?" and he went back, swung her into his arms and kissed her. For comfort, he told himself, that was all…

But when she rose on her toes, wound her arms around his neck and kissed him back, he knew damned well that comfort was the last thing on his mind.

CHAPTER FIVE

SHE'D thought he was going to walk away.

That was what she wanted. If he left her alone, maybe she could figure out what had happened to her. She couldn't do that with Jesse Blackwolf's dark eyes watching her, judging her, trying to figure out what kind of game she was playing.

But when he really had started to leave, a terrible loneliness had threatened to swallow her up. *Jesse,* she'd said, without knowing she was going to say it…and when he came back and took her in his arms, she'd realized that loneliness wasn't the reason she'd called him back.

He was the reason.

She barely knew this man…and yet, in a way that made no sense at all, she felt as if she'd known him forever.

She sighed with pleasure when his arms closed around her. His body was hard and strong, his heartbeat steady beneath her ear. Of everything that had happened to her in the past endless hours, this, only this, was real.

Jesse's embrace. His scent. The feel of him against her.

"Jesse," she said again, and raised her face to his, willing his lips to take hers. To chase away the internal darkness that threatened to consume her.

She wasn't a thief, she wasn't even a trespasser, because there weren't any No Trespassing signs around the endless acres of Jesse's land.

Not on June 21, 2010.

Except—except Jesse said it wasn't 2010. It was 1975, he'd said, and she'd either stepped through the looking glass like Alice…

Or she'd lost her mind. She was moments from stepping into a darkness as deep as the canyon.

And only Jesse could save her.

His kiss was gentle, the light brush of mouth against mouth.

"Shh," he said softly. "Shh, baby."

He was trying to soothe her but it wasn't enough. She wanted more and she sought his mouth again, slid her hands up his chest. Her fingers brushed over the eagle talon; it seemed hot with an almost mystical energy, but the heat of his skin was masculine and real, the muscles beneath pronounced and taut. An electric shudder went through him at her touch and sent an answering tremor of response sizzling along each of her nerve endings. He groaned; the sound made her heart beat faster. Blind to everything but the moment, Sienna rose on her toes, pressed the length of her body against Jesse's and dug her hands into the silky hair that fell loose around his face.

His erection was instantaneous, hard and powerful and life-affirming as it nudged unashamedly against her belly. She moaned into his mouth and moved against him.

He said something against her parted lips. The words were guttural and she didn't understand them, but she understood the urgency in his voice, the urgency in her quickening blood.

The sheet slipped and fell to the floor. Naked now, her entire body tight against his, she moaned again as he cupped her bottom, lifted her into him.

His erection felt huge. Enormous. His heat radiated through her body.

Real. Yes. Oh, yes. This was not a dream, not a hallucination. His hand was between her thighs, seeking, finding her. His mouth was at her breast, sucking her nipple deep into his mouth.

She clung to him, her hands deep in his hair as he swept her up and carried her quickly into the darkness beyond the bright pool of light. They tumbled onto the bed, mouths fused.

She needed him. Wanted him. Her heart was racing with the hot urgency of desire as he settled over her, his welcome weight pressing her down into the softness of his bed. He pushed down her panties; she felt him doing the same with his sweats.

In a moment, he would be deep inside her. This man. This stranger.

This stranger!

Sienna's eyes flew open. "Wait," she said breathlessly. "Jesse, wait!"

He clasped her face as she tried to twist it from his, held her still and kissed her.

"No. Jesse. Please! I don't want to—"

He wasn't listening. For all she knew, he couldn't even hear her. Breath sobbing in and out of her lungs, she shoved hard at his chest.

"Jesse," she gasped. "Listen to me!"

She beat at his shoulders and he caught her wrists, dragged her arms high above her head, forced his knee between her thighs.

"No! Jesse, no, no, no…"

His big body stilled. Then he let go of her wrists, rolled away and got to his feet.

Naked, without his body covering hers, a cold as deep as

the surrounding darkness settled against Sienna's skin. Her teeth chattered; she rolled onto her side. Something fell over her. Terry cloth. A robe? Whatever it was, she covered herself with it and scrambled up against the pillows. Light blazed down. She threw up a hand to shield her eyes and saw Jesse standing over her, the lantern in his hand.

Half naked, his sweats hanging low on his hips, he stood motionless. His hair was loose and hung to his jaw. He'd wiped away the black stripes, but the eagle talon still swung from its rawhide thong. He was, somehow, a remarkable mixture of savagery and civilization, wild and dangerous…

And incredibly beautiful.

Heat rushed through her. What would it have been like to have felt him possessing her?

"That's a risky game to play," he said in a low voice.

Her eyes flew to his. "It wasn't a game," she said, rushing the words. "I never meant—" Sienna hesitated. She wanted to blame what had happened on him but she couldn't. "Everything—everything's confused," she said in a tremulous whisper. "There's so much going on…." She swallowed. "I'm sorry."

He gave a harsh laugh. "Yeah. So am I."

"I don't—I don't know what…what happened. I'm not—"

"Frankly, I don't give a damn what you are or aren't. You won't be here long enough for it to mean anything. As soon as the storm ends, I want you off my land."

She nodded. It was what she wanted, too. Somewhere out there, people had to be missing her. Looking for her…

"Get some clothes on. There's stuff in the dressing room." He leaned forward and placed the lantern on the nightstand. "I'll be in the kitchen, putting together something to eat."

"Really, that's not nec—"

"I decide what's necessary around here, lady. Get that through your head."

"Jesse. Mr. Blackwolf—"

"Put on a couple of layers of clothing. Without power, it's going to be a long, cold night."

Sienna nodded, watching as he headed for the door. Stupid, she knew, but the thought of him vanishing into the dark in this unknown place made her uneasy.

"Wait!"

He swung toward her. "What now?"

"The light. Don't you need it?"

He reached for the candle. "This will do me just fine."

The door slammed after him, and Sienna was alone.

She waited for what seemed a very long.

The question wasn't would he come back, but would her legs hold her when she stood up? She felt shaky. That she'd come within a heartbeat of letting a hard-edged stranger who thought she was some kind of thief almost take her to bed seemed impossible....

Sienna let out a shaky breath.

Be honest, at least!

Jesse Blackwolf hadn't been the aggressor. She'd been as eager as he. She'd wanted him to make love to her, wanted him more than she'd ever wanted a man before. Not that there'd been many to start with. A boy in her junior year at college, another at the start of her postgraduate studies—her sex life was pretty pathetic by 2010 standards.

How about by the standards of 1975? She tried to remember what she knew of sex in the seventies. Free love? Sexual equality?

Not that it mattered.

She'd reacted to Jesse on her own terms, not those of any particular year or era. His touch, his taste, the feel of him against her...

She shut her eyes, let herself remember it all. The texture of his silky hair, the hard planes of his shoulders and chest, the press of his erection. The heat, the warmth of his kisses.

Desire, something so potent she couldn't think of a name for it, had caught her in its grasp. All she'd wanted was to be in Jesse's arms, to know what it was like to belong to him....

"Stop it," she said sharply.

She wasn't like that; she didn't want to be like that. Sex had a place in a woman's life and that was exactly the way it should be, it should have a *place* in a woman's life. End of story.

What had just happened was nothing but the end result of a day that had started in one time and ended in another, and no, absolutely no, she was not going to think about that now!

Sienna sat up, pulled on the robe—Jesse's, of course. She could tell by the size, which dwarfed her. By the scent, redolent of mountain air, pine and man. Then she headed for the dressing room, lantern in her hand....

And stopped in the doorway. She hadn't really looked at the room before, when she'd fled here. Now she saw that it was huge, easily as big as her Brooklyn apartment.

Except, her place overflowed with, well, with just plain stuff.

Jesse's dressing room was so close to empty, it was Spartan.

Shelves and cubbies lined the walls, but most of them were empty. Only a couple of narrow sections contained clothes. A couple of wool sport jackets hung from a rack; jeans, sweaters, T-shirts, sweats—tops and bottoms—were all neatly folded and neatly aligned on the shelves. Boxer shorts and socks were alongside.

At the far end of the room, in lonely splendor, a military

uniform hung suspended from a hanger on a rod. A pair of boots, polished to a gleaming luster, stood directly beneath.

Sienna set the lantern on an empty shelf. Was her reluctant host a soldier? It was none of her business. Still, she crossed the room for a closer look.

Her breath caught.

The jacket bristled with medals and ribbons. She had no idea what any of them were; she didn't even know what branch of service the uniform represented, but whatever it was, Jesse must have served it well.

She couldn't imagine him as a soldier. He was too independent to take orders from anyone. He was good at giving orders, though....

She jumped as a fist banged against the still-shut outer door.

"Hurry it up," Jesse barked.

Sienna almost laughed. "Yessir," she said, and gave the all-but-empty room a brisk salute.

The kitchen was easy to find.

The lantern provided plenty of light and all she had to do was follow the smell of...

"Chicken noodle soup?"

Jesse turned as she entered the candlelit room. He'd put on a long-sleeved chambray shirt, the sleeves rolled back on his tanned, muscled forearms. He was wearing a fresh pair of jeans and his hair was drawn back from his face and secured with a length of rawhide. He stood at a marble counter over a pot bubbling away on the burner of a camping stove, a wooden spoon in his hand, a noncommittal expression on his face, and gave her a long look.

"I see you found something to wear."

Sienna glanced down at herself. She was wearing heavy

gray cotton sweats—classic, basic gymwear. There'd been half a dozen pair in the dressing room, varying only as to color. Jesse was apparently not given to anything that defeated the utilitarian purpose of sweats, or to silly designer logos.

She couldn't imagine he ever would be.

"Yes." She decided to test the waters, offer a small flag of truce by giving him a hesitant smile. "I took your advice about layering. I have on two of your T-shirts. And—" she raised one foot "—two pairs of socks."

"Good." He swung back to the stove. "You can put the lantern over there."

"Okay." He heard the soft scuff of her sock-clad feet as she made her way across the Mexican-tile floor. "The soup smells wonderful."

"I opened two cans. There's plenty of it."

"Good. Anything I can do?"

Yeah, he thought. There was.

She could stop looking so beautiful.

He had to be really desperate, he thought coldly, finding Sienna Cummings beautiful. Not that there was anything wrong with her looks; it was just that he didn't go for her type. Independent women, questioning women, ones who thought they were on an equal footing with men...

Not that he liked his women stupid.

He just liked them to know when to defer to a man.

He wasn't into this women's lib nonsense that had taken the country by storm.

Linda hadn't been into it, either. She'd known how to make a man feel good. She'd looked up to him, let him know he was in charge....

Until he suddenly hadn't been.

I need a man who knows how to be a man, Jesse, she'd said, and how could he fault her for that? A woman didn't want a man in her bed who woke up soaked to the skin from nightmares that kept threatening to pull him under, who had no clue as to what he wanted to do with his life, who had believed with all his being in things that no longer made sense....

"...must be something I can do," Sienna said, and he blinked and focused his eyes on her.

"What?"

"I said, you did the cooking. I'd like to do something. Set the table, maybe?"

"I opened a can," he said gruffly.

"Two."

She smiled. It was impossible not to smile back.

"Yeah. Okay." He jerked his head toward one of the birch cupboards. "How about setting the counter? The bowls are in there. Silverware's in that drawer, bread's in that cabinet. You want butter, there's some in the fridge. Just don't keep the door open longer than you have to."

"Yessir."

Jesse narrowed his eyes. "What's that supposed to mean?"

"Nothing." She hesitated. "It just, you know, slipped out. I mean, I saw your uniform. It was just hanging there. Look, I didn't mean to pry...."

"Then don't," he said sharply. "Just give me those bowls."

The look she flashed would have made him laugh if he'd been in a better mood, but he wasn't in a better mood and all she got in return was a glare.

She slapped the bowls on the counter beside him. He ladled the soup into them, then turned off the camping stove.

"I was in the army," he said flatly. "Okay?"

"Fine."

"Now, sit down and eat."

She took one of the high-backed stools, dipped her spoon into the bowl he put before her…and cleared her throat.

"That didn't look like a regular army uniform. I mean, those boots. And that hat on the shelf…"

"And what do you know about regular army uniforms?"

"We had ROTC on campus."

"Yeah," he said with biting sarcasm, "Reserve Officers' Training Corps. Well, that sure makes you an expert."

"Look, if you don't want to talk about it—"

"I was in Special Forces." His tone was not only flat, it was icy. "Any more questions?"

Sienna shook her head. He was right, she was prying, and it was none of her business.

"Fine. Now, eat your soup."

"Any other orders you want to give, General?"

"Wrong rank," he said curtly. "And I'm not giving you orders, I'm just telling you what to do."

Her eyebrows rose. Who could blame her? He knew he sounded like an idiot.

"Okay," he said, "okay, I'm not good at this."

"At what?" Her smile was as sickly sweet as her voice. "At behaving like a human being?"

"At having anybody here. This place…I spend most of my time here alone."

"What a surprise."

"I'm not much for company."

Another of those sugar-on-overload smiles. "I'd never have guessed."

He looked at her. There was that attitude again. Women weren't supposed to be like that. They weren't supposed to have that do-I-strike-you-as-a-pushover thing going on—but then, he'd never known a woman like this one.

This was, no question, turning into an interesting experience. Except he didn't want an interesting experience. He'd had enough of those to last a lifetime.

"Just eat the soup." He pushed a plate piled high with slices of white bread toward her. "Bread, too. You burned up a lot of calories today."

He could almost hear her thinking of a way to refute what he'd said, just as a matter of principle. But she was too smart for that. Despite her earlier claim about not being hungry, she was. She needed food; she knew it, he knew it, and after a couple of seconds she shrugged, picked up her spoon and dug in.

She ate all her soup. Four slices of bread. When she finished, she licked her lips.

"That was delicious."

He nodded, folded his sixth piece of bread in half and bit into it.

"I am," he said, "one hell of a gourmet cook."

She looked at him. Then, slowly, her lips curved into a smile. It was, he thought, a great smile, the kind that didn't seem painted on just to make a man feel good. Not that there was anything wrong with a woman doing whatever it took to make a man feel good, it was only that honest smiles were rare.

"I can see that," she said somberly, "you and a lady named Mrs. Campbell."

"Hey," he said, trying to sound as if she'd injured his pride, "it takes special talent to turn a can of soup into five stars in the *Michelin Guide*."

She laughed. "Tell me about it. I do a lot of that kind of gourmet cooking, too."

"Ah."

"Ah, indeed."

He looked at her, then away. "I take it Jack doesn't do kitchen duty?"

"Jack?"

"The guy. The one you were with."

Her smile faded. "Oh. That Jack."

"Is there another?"

"No. I mean…" She frowned, found a breadcrumb on the counter and toyed with it. "For a little while there, I forgot."

"About Jack?"

Her head came up. "What's with the Jack thing? Why would I think about him?"

"Because he's your lover," Jesse said, his voice gone hard.

"My lover? Jack?" Her tone was incredulous.

"What is he, then?"

"My professor. Well, he isn't a full professor, but I'm working on my thesis with him."

"A thesis in…"

Her expression turned defiant. "Anthropology. Native American peoples."

"You mean, Indians."

"I mean Native Americans. That word, Indian, is an insult—"

"That's news to me. Besides, do I look insulted?"

Sienna stared at him. What he looked was proud. And so beautiful it put an ache in her throat.

What if this Jesse was real? If he was the man she'd read about and wondered about? What if this was, as he kept insisting, reality?

It was impossible. *This* was impossible. She couldn't dwell on it or she'd—she'd tumble off the edge of the earth and who knew where she'd land?

Her stool squealed in protest as she shoved it back, got to her feet and snatched up their spoons and bowls.

"I'm an anthropologist," she said steadily. "Jack Burden is my adviser. That's what brought me to this place." She moved swiftly from the counter to the sink, dumping the dishes and cutlery, returning to grab the loaf of bread and close the wrapper. She'd started her response to him calmly, but she could feel emotion building inside her. "I didn't come to steal, or to deface things or to trespass on your land. I came to study something ancient and—and wonderful and amazing, and I resent—"

Jesse rose from his seat.

"Okay," he said quietly.

"No. No, it's not okay." She looked up at him, but between the bad lighting and the angry tears that had risen in her eyes, her vision was blurry. "It's not okay for you to accuse me of—of such awful things. I am not—"

"I said, okay. You're not."

"Not what?" she said, her voice shaking. "Not here? Not standing in a room that doesn't exist, with a man who doesn't ex—"

"I exist," he said roughly, and despite all the promises he'd made himself and her, he took her into his arms and raised her face to his. "I exist, Sienna," he said softly. "You know it and so do I."

Her eyes met his. They glittered with unshed tears but, he was certain, with something else, too.

Awareness.

Of him.

Of herself.

Of the electricity between them.

Jesse raised his hand and stroked an errant curl back from her temple. She turned her head like a cat moving deeper into what could easily become a caress.

All he had to do was bend his head and kiss her. One kiss and she'd melt into his arms.

Make love to me, Jesse, she would whisper, and this time, she'd mean it. No games. No last-minute recriminations. No backing away from what they both wanted.

"Jesse?"

Her eyes were wide and luminous. Her lips were parted in anticipation. He thought of that uniform, hanging in his dressing room. Of a time, an eternity ago, when he had been an officer and a gentleman.

And took a step back.

"Take the lantern," he said gruffly. She didn't move; he grabbed it and shoved it at her. "Go on, take it. There are extra blankets in the chest at the foot of the bed. Pile them on. You'll need them."

"But where will you sleep?"

He wouldn't. Not with her just down the hall.

"I'll bunk in the living room. By the fireplace."

"Yes, but—"

"Damn it," he growled, "must you fight me on everything?"

That don't-screw-with-me look was back on her face. He wanted to pull her to him and kiss it away. Instead, he folded his arms, glared at her until she muttered a very unladylike word, turned her back and marched off. At the last minute, just before the dark swallowed her up, he called her name.

"Sienna." She stopped, but she didn't turn around. "Lock your door," he said, his voice as rough as sandpaper. "And keep it locked."

Then he looked away from her, tucked his hands into the back pockets of his jeans and stared blindly out the window into the deep black night that had finally embraced the house.

CHAPTER SIX

WAS he watching her as she went down the dark hall?

Sienna wanted to run but instinct warned her against it.

You didn't run from a predator. You stood up tall and showed no fear, and that was important here. Jesse had deliberately tried to scare her, she was sure of it.

But he couldn't.

She wasn't afraid of him. Or of what had just happened between them. The excitement of his hands on her. The way he'd looked at her. The wild storm raging outside, the even wilder storm just waiting to break free inside….

By the time she was halfway to the bedroom, her heart was doing its best to leap from her chest. Only another few feet, she told herself; she was almost there. All she had to do was keep up the pose. Head high, shoulders back, steps steady. Now to open the door. Good. Step through it. Fine.

"Oh, God," she whispered, and she slammed the door, locked it with trembling fingers, fell back against the cool wood and took a long, ragged breath.

How dare this man do this to her? What gave him the right to try to frighten her to death?

Lock your door. What was she supposed to be? His slave?

And for what? Did he honestly think he'd needed to tell her to safeguard herself against him after that take-no-prisoners kiss?

A man who kissed a woman as Jesse had kissed her was dangerous.

And a woman who responded to such a kiss was in deep trouble.

Sienna swallowed dryly.

No. She had not responded. She was—she was in pieces, emotionally. He knew it. He'd taken advantage of her but it would not happen again.

Really? How many times can you kiss him back and still tell yourself it's not your doing, that you're not actually responding?

The whisper inside her was sly. And brutally honest.

Okay. What she had to do was get control of things. Calm down. Take deep breaths. In. Out. Good. And again. Very good. See? It was working. Her heart was slowing. Only a thousand beats per minute instead of a million, she thought on a nervous laugh.

Laughing was good, even if it was shaky. It meant she was thinking again instead of simply reacting.

If only the storm would stop. If the lights would come on. At least she had the lantern and its bright glow. The only thing wrong with that was that it cast such a brilliant glow that it made the darkness pooled beyond it all the more absolute. She could see nothing beyond the bed. The windows were blank and black.

Not good.

Resolutely, she crossed the room, put the lantern on the night table, hurried to the windows and shut the vertical blinds.

Much better.

There was something about the night pressing in that was disturbing…but not as disturbing as Jesse Blackwolf. He was the proverbial enigma wrapped in a paradox, a beautiful, sleek, powerful mystery. He thought she'd trespassed on his property, that she'd come to steal artifacts, but he'd still risked his neck getting her down that mountain. He'd brought her here, taken care of her, fed her…

And kissed her.

He could have done more.

For a moment, for a heartbeat, he could have done anything he'd wanted. She'd known it. So had he.

But he hadn't. Why? Why had he let her go, let her put a locked door between them? Not that a lock would stop him. If he came for her, the door would be a meaningless barrier. And once he'd broken it down, she'd be defenseless. He'd strip her of the oversized clothing, carry her to his bed, take her again and again and again….

Excitement shimmered within her.

Was that what she wanted? To be ravished? To have no choice except to give in to him? To have his mouth hot on her skin, his hands exploring her? To feel his hard body against hers?

Possessing her.

Sienna sank down on the edge of the bed and pressed her fingertips to her temples. Maybe she really was going crazy. A kiss. That was all it was…though, when you came down to it, maybe it hadn't been a kiss at all. Maybe it had been a raw declaration of power. Men were still into those things in the 1970s….

Assuming this was the 1970s and not some white-walled room in an Intensive Care Unit. Or the local psycho ward.

"Enough," she said, and sprang to her feet.

She wasn't going there. It was enough to understand why he'd kissed her. Never mind the decade or even the century. Men were men. The *I'm-male-you're-female-and-that's-that* routine was in their DNA and would probably remain there forever.

The key to sanity was to think logically. Concentrate on practicalities. Like the fact that she knew her name even if she wasn't so sure about the date. Or that if she pinched herself—"Ouch!"—if she did, it hurt.

So, she was fine with the basics.

She was also in one piece. She had hot soup in her belly. She was dry. And warm. Well, fairly warm, not outside in the cold and the wet.

And the door was locked against Jesse.

He couldn't get to her. Couldn't take her in his arms again. Kiss her. Caress her. Make her blood run thick and hot…

She drew a long breath. What she needed was sleep—but not in this bed. Not under Jesse's blankets or with her head on his pillows. No way. Damned if she understood why that seemed so important, but it did.

There was a big armchair by the window. All she had to do was turn it so it faced into the room, like that, then settle into it, like this. Shut her eyes and sleep. When she awoke, it would be morning.

Things had a way of looking lots better by daylight.

But the chair, while big, wasn't comfortable. Not as a substitute bed. She couldn't stretch out or do anything with her legs except tuck them up under her, and that wasn't so good because her thighs and calves ached. The climb down the mountain had taken its toll. She couldn't lean her head back, either. The final insult was that after a few minutes of sitting still, the sweats and socks she was wearing didn't feel quite so warm.

She eyed the duvet, then rolled her eyes. Ridiculous, to sit here with her teeth chattering. A blanket was a blanket, nothing more, and she reached for it, yanked it over herself and all but moaned as she wrapped up in its voluminous folds.

But it wasn't enough. Five minutes and she could feel the cold seeping in.

So what?

Was she a wuss or a woman?

Not a wuss, she thought determinedly. She'd practically raised herself, her father a bullying drunk who barked orders, her mother a pathetic creature who followed those orders blindly. Somehow, she'd survived, found academic opportunities in a high school so low on the educational totem pole that when she graduated from it with a scholarship to Columbia University, not even she'd believed it. And when her major in Business had turned out to be a mistake, who'd had the courage to talk the Powers That Be into letting her keep the scholarship despite switching her major to Anthro?

"Me," she said into the silence.

Spending the night in a chair? A piece of cake. So what if it was a little chilly? She just had to stop thinking so much. About what in hell was happening to her…

About Jesse. Jesse, the enigma.

Good looking. Well spoken. And heroic. He had a spit-and-polish uniform in his dressing room but he went around half naked, paint on his face, riding hell-bent for leather without a saddle.

She'd never seen him in that uniform, but she knew damned well he'd look magnificent. Whatever he wore, whoever he was, Special Forces officer or Native-American warrior, he'd be gorgeous. And sexy. And spectacularly sexy…

Sienna moaned and shut her eyes. Sleep. She needed sleep. Maybe if she turned off the lantern…

"Woman or wuss?" she said briskly, and she reached for the Coleman lamp, doused the flame and plunged the room into darkness.

* * *

Jesse was awake, pacing the living room at the far end of the house by the light of a dying fire.

He hadn't noticed it was dying. How could he when his brain was focused on what had just happened? On what he'd done, damned near forcing himself on a woman who didn't want him….

Except she did.

Oh, yes. She'd wanted him as much as he'd wanted her.

He came to a stop, folded his arms, glowered at the shadows the flames cast on the walls. What he needed was some rest.

Yeah, but how to get it?

He'd tried the sofa. Too narrow. The floor. Too hard. The Eames chair and ottoman by the windows. Too uncomfortable. He felt like a pathetic version of Goldilocks and there wasn't a thing he could do about it except mutter and curse and grumble over his inability to catch some desperately needed shut-eye, and maybe try and find some humor in the fact that he was a man who'd never had that kind of problem before.

As a kid, he'd learned to sleep in the open, never mind the weather. A sleeping bag had been all he'd needed; that was his old man's sole concession to his mother on overnight hunting and fishing trips into the mountains.

And when he'd grown up, enlisted in the army, volunteered and made it into Special Forces… Those sleeping bag excursions had turned into memories of luxury as they'd given way to bug-infested jungles and muddy holes in the ground and, if he was really lucky, caves that still stunk of whatever critters had last sought shelter inside them.

All he'd had to do was shut his eyes, set his internal clock for a wake-up call in twenty minutes or two hours and he was gone, even with Charlie someplace out there.

But Charlie was gone. There was no enemy here at all.

There was, instead, a woman. And knowing she was in his bedroom, curled up in his bed while he was out here, was keeping him wide-awake.

Unless he wasn't actually tired.

"Bull," he muttered as he strode past the fireplace again.

Hell, he was exhausted. A man made poor decisions when his body and mind were worn out. But that kiss, that kiss…

Jesse muttered a sharp expletive and kicked a glowing coal back onto the hearth.

And he was stuck with her. He wouldn't have turned a field mouse out on a night like this. Tomorrow, first thing, absolutely, he'd send her on her way, but for now—for now, he had no choice but to give her shelter.

The fire was burning down. He'd forgotten to feed it. He'd forgotten more than that since Sienna Cummings turned up, he thought grimly.

What had become of logic? Of self-control? Why in hell had he kissed her just now? Not once. Twice. And that second time, all restraint gone…

He squatted before the hearth, added wood, poked at the glowing embers until the new logs caught with tendrils of orange flame.

Okay. He'd already gone through this. He needed a woman. A soft female body beneath his. He was a man, with a man's instincts, and living like a hermit was not a good thing…but that wasn't enough to explain what had happened.

Kissing a woman the way he'd kissed this one…

His intruder.

His beautiful intruder.

His terrified intruder.

And she was that. Terrified. Not of having been caught

stealing. She wasn't a thief. He knew that now. She was scared of something else, something more….

But not of him.

When he'd kissed her she'd kissed him back. Melted in his arms, her mouth hot on his. He could have taken her then….

The storm was still raging, the power was off, the roads were undoubtedly blocked and here he was, pacing like a caged tiger, getting himself as worked up as a schoolboy and over what?

A kiss.

He had more important things to worry about. The horses, for instance. He hadn't given them a thought in hours.

Lightning flashed outside the window as he headed for the kitchen, shoved his feet into dry boots, grabbed a rain slicker and a flashlight, then went out the back door at a trot. There were only a few animals in the barn and most had calm dispositions, but the intensity of the storm might have spooked them. He'd talk to them, feed them. That was lots better than wasting time thinking about a woman he'd never see after tomorrow.

Keeping busy was, as always, the ticket to success.

The horses were fine.

They whinnied their greetings, butted velvet noses against his shoulder as he went from stall to stall. He gave them buckets of oats, dug a handful of mints from a box near the door, gave each animal the much-coveted treat, refilled water buckets, spoke softly and reassuringly. A barn cat meowed for attention and wound sinuously around his ankles; he bent down, stroked it, smiled at its thousand-decibel purr.

Eventually, despite his best efforts, there was nothing left to do but return to the house.

He dripped water over the mudroom floor, hung up the slicker, toed off his boots and headed for the living room. The house was cold and getting colder by the minute. Even the warm spot before the fireplace seemed narrower than before.

What about the bedroom? It had to be like Siberia.

So what? Sienna had his robe. His bed. She was warm enough. Besides, that wasn't his problem. He'd given her food, shelter, something dry to wear….

"Hell," he muttered, and headed down the dark hall, candle in hand.

He'd knock. Wait for her response. Better to wake her than run the risk of letting her freeze off that cute little ass.

He reached the bedroom door. Took a couple of breaths. Knocked. Nothing. He knocked again. "Sienna?" No reply. He tried again, louder this time. "Sienna? Are you okay?"

Still nothing.

Jesse started to turn away. A muscle jumped in his jaw. He tried the doorknob but she'd followed orders and thrown the bolt.

What he hadn't bothered mentioning was that the bolt didn't always work.

He blew out the candle and entered the room quietly. He didn't want to scare her, he only wanted to make sure she was all right.

The room was dark as pitch—she'd closed the verticals. A protective instinct; he understood it even if he'd never have followed it. Being able to see the enemy coming was vital to survival.

It took a few minutes until his vision adjusted. Still, the soft sound of her breathing, the delicate scent of woman and wildflowers told him where she was before he saw her.

Jesse narrowed his eyes. Not that he gave a damn about any of that. The point was, she hadn't done as he'd told her, after all. Instead of getting into bed and piling on the blankets, she'd fallen asleep in a chair. She looked uncomfortable, her head tilted at an awkward angle, her long legs tucked under her. And she had to be cold. The room was cold enough for him to see the exhalations of his breath.

"Sienna," he said sharply. She sighed, shifted in her sleep. Grinding his teeth, he put the back of his hand to her cheek and swore under his breath. Her skin was almost painfully cool.

"Idiot," he muttered, but the word lacked conviction. She wasn't stupid. She was proud. Independent. Determined to do things on her own terms. God knew, he could relate to that.

Well, he'd run out of choices. He had to do what was logical. What necessity demanded. Take her out of this refrigerator and keep her warm.

Scooping her into his arms, duvet and all, was easy. She was light, boneless, and though she made a little sound of protest, she didn't awaken as he carried her from the room. Her head fell against his shoulder. Her hair tickled his nose, and he gave in to the urge to inhale its fragrance as he made his way to the living room.

He put her on the sofa, grabbed a couple of the blankets he'd left her earlier and arranged three of them on the floor before the hearth, spread the remaining two over the improvised mattress and folded them back. Then he gathered Sienna in his arms and lay down with her against him, both of them wrapped in the duvet and now covered, too, by the soft wool blankets.

His actions were brisk. Purposeful. As if making a bed by the fire, settling into it with a woman in his arms, was everyday stuff.

He'd forgotten pillows. It didn't matter. He could do without one and Sienna… Sienna sighed and put her head on his shoulder.

He went very still.

Another sigh. She flung her arm over his chest, her leg over his. He could feel the race of his heart.

"Sienna," he said, and cleared his throat, "Sienna…"

She moved closer. Her hair whispered like silk against his jaw. Sweet Lord, she was killing him!

Okay. Enough. He could do this. Roll her off him. Put some space between them. Not too much; she needed his body heat but—

"Jesse?"

Her voice was as soft as a summer breeze. Her eyes opened and met his. His heart thundered when she smiled.

"Yeah." He cleared his throat again. "The bedroom's too cold. I couldn't leave you there. You're safe here. I promise I won't—"

"Jesse. You came for me."

He told himself she was half asleep. That she was dreaming. He kept telling it to himself even as she wound her arms around his neck.

"Sienna…"

He bit back a groan. Her skin had gone from chilled to hot; her hands were like flame on his shoulders. He wanted to kiss her. Put his lips to hers, see if she really tasted as sweet as she had before.

She did.

Sweet. Honeyed. And tender. God, so tender, the fit of her mouth so perfect under his.

Her breath hitched. "Jesse," she whispered. "Jesse…"

This was when a decent man would have stopped. Pulled back and said, *Sienna, baby, you don't know what you're doing.*

But he wasn't a decent man, he hadn't been one in a very long time. And when she framed his face with her hands and lifted herself to him, when she bit lightly at his bottom lip, he gave up thinking, rolled her beneath him and took the kiss as deep and savage as the storm that raged outside.

CHAPTER SEVEN

SIENNA had slept, but badly.

Frightening dreams that left her on the knife-edge of panic kept waking her. Or maybe it was the cold, seeping into her bones. She'd been able to see her breath condensing in the increasingly cold room.

Foolish, not to have climbed into Jesse's bed, she'd thought, but by the time she admitted it, the effort to do it seemed too great and she'd tumbled back into uneasy sleep.

Then, as if in a dream, she'd heard Jesse speak her name. Felt his arms closing around her, carrying her away from the cold room, from her nightmares, bringing her to warmth and safety simply because he held her.

And then he kissed her.

The kiss roused her from sleep, sent delicious shock waves coursing through her body, made her feel alive and secure....

Made her want more.

She came fully awake, aware that he was holding her as if she were made of glass, his powerful body taut with awareness, as if he knew he could crush her at any moment.

But restraint wasn't what she wanted.

She wanted Jesse, his hunger, his desire. She wanted the oblivion she knew he could bring her.

"Jesse," she said, and wound her arms around his neck, lifted herself to him. And when she sensed him still holding back, she brought her mouth to his and nipped at his lip.

His reaction was as swift as her racing heart.

He groaned like a man in pain, rolled her onto her back and took command.

He plunged his hands into her hair, framed her face, brought it to his. No gentle kiss as it had been before. This time, his lips were hungry and demanding. His breathing was ragged. Hers was, too. She heard herself making soft moans of impassioned longing.

He slid one arm beneath her and raised her against him.

Yes. Oh, yes. The heavy thrust of his erection against her belly was the best possible affirmation that all of this was really happening.

Her eyes flew open when he pulled back the blanket.

"Don't stop," she said, "please, Jesse, don't—"

"Are you sure?"

She nodded. "Very sure."

His eyes darkened. "I want to see you."

His voice was low and rough and so sexy she thought she might come just from hearing it. Her hands went to the hem of her sweatshirt and she began to lift it.

"No," he said in that same gruff whisper. "I'll do it."

He pushed her hands aside and slowly, so slowly she thought she might die, he drew the shirt over her head and tossed it aside.

He smiled. "I almost forgot those two T-shirts," he said softly.

And stripped them away, as well.

His smile faded. His gaze fell to her breasts. The look he gave her now was everything a woman could ever ask for from her lover. It was as hot, as filled with dangerous promise, as the fire.

She felt her nipples tighten, her breasts lift with desire. He had yet to touch her. Still, she had never before been so aware of her body's reactions to a man.

But then, there'd never been a man like Jesse.

The feeling was exciting. Even frightening. She wanted it never, ever to stop.

"Jesse?" she whispered.

He raised his head. Her breath caught. His beautiful face was all bones and angles and sharply etched planes. He looked at her for what seemed like forever, and then, eyes on hers, he touched his hand to her breast. One soft touch, the brush of his knuckles over her nipple.

A sob burst from her throat.

"It's too much," she said. "Jesse, Jesse…"

His thumb whispered over the taut bud. Once. Twice. Again. Sienna sobbed his name. Caught his hand but he ignored her, gently pushed her hand aside and went on stroking her, touching her before, slowly, he dipped his head and put his mouth to her other breast. Her other nipple. Sucked it into his hot, wet mouth.

"Jesse, please. I'm going to—I'm going to—"

The world stopped.

She gave a cry as wild as the storm and Jesse growled her name, lifted his head and took possession of her mouth, swallowing her cry of completion, making it a part of him as she came apart in his arms, her body weeping with desire.

She gasped his name. Pulled at his shirt. He said something low and urgent, pushed her hands away, tore at the shirt himself. She heard buttons pop, fabric tear, and then his skin was against hers, all that heat, that hard muscle, the faint abrasion of his hair-roughened chest. She moved her hands over him with feverish determination, loving the feel of him. The wide shoulders, the sculpted biceps, the abs that might have been chiseled from stone.

She'd wanted to lose herself, but something more was happening here. Something she had not expected and—and—

"Lift up," he whispered, and she did, and he pulled down her sweatpants and now…

Now she was completely naked in his arms.

"Sienna."

He whispered her name against her mouth. Her throat. Her breasts. His hand cupped one breast, his fingers deliciously calloused against the sensitive nipple, then moved down her side, shaping her waist, her hip, her thigh. She cried out. It was too much. Too much. Too…

And then his hand was between her thighs and Sienna stopped thinking and fell headlong into sensation.

Sensation. He was drowning in it. Sienna's taste. The silk of her skin. The hammer of her heart, the soft cries she made as he touched her. And the scent of her body, musky and aroused and so exciting he could feel himself starting to slide over the edge.

Jesse shut his eyes, breathed deep, fought for control. He couldn't let this end so quickly. He knew there were times sex should be fast, times it could be hot and quick….

But not this time.

The woman in his arms was wild and beautiful, and he wanted the taking of her, the giving of himself, to go on forever.

But he wanted her. Her soft mouth. Her sweet nipples. That hidden bud in her body's feminine delta that he could kiss and taste as it flowered, as he brought her the release she deserved.

She'd come once, but he wanted it to happen again and again, until she was exhausted, until she lay beneath him knowing him, only him, no other man but him.

He knew that kind of thinking was dangerous…and then it was too late to think. All he could do was kiss her. Let her taste fill him.

Honey. Cream. Her skin, her lips. He moved down her body, caressing her everywhere, groaning at the feel of her hands on him. He pressed a kiss to her belly, and when he tried to put his mouth even lower she dug her hands into his hair, dragged his face up to hers.

He let her do it. Took her mouth. Stroked his tongue against hers. Let her set the pace, but he needed more.

She whispered his name.

Her hips rose. Pressed against him. Moved against him.

He could feel the earth slipping away. On a low growl, he swept one hand beneath her, raised her to him despite her shocked gasp, used his fingers to seek the very heart of her.

A brush of his thumb and she moaned. Another stroke; she cried out. He brought his mouth to her, kissed her hungrily, a man thirsting for a life-sustaining drink after a long, endless drought, and she gave a long, broken cry and came against his mouth.

"Yes," he said, "yes, baby. Like that. Like that, for me. Only for me."

He kissed her breasts, her throat, lingered in the delicate hollow, felt the way her pulse raced against his lips. Kissed her collarbone, the elegant slope of her breast. Kissed her nipples, tongued them, sucked them deep into his mouth, sweat beading on his forehead from the effort of not taking her.

He knew he would not last long, once he was inside her; he was a man who never lost control, but he was close to losing it now.

"Jesse," she sobbed, "Jesse, Jesse…"

The sound of his name on her tongue filled him with elation.

"Tell me," he said fiercely. "Tell me what you want."

"You. You!" Her hands fumbled at his belt. "Jesse. Please. Please. I want—"

All at once, the harsh light of a thousand suns filled the room. The power was back, and the lights had come on. Every damned one of them.

The huge glass-and-copper chandelier in the entrance to the living room. The spots over the sofa. The alabaster lamps on the glass tables flanking the sofa. Lights blazed everywhere, offering brutal illumination to the most intimate moment a man and woman can share.

Sienna cried out and threw her hand in front of her eyes. Jesse clasped that hand, folded her fingers into her palm.

"Easy," he said.

She stared at him, eyes wide with shock. He'd seen the reaction before, once in a doe frozen by his sudden appearance deep in a wooded valley, and more times than he wanted to remember in the faces of men who'd thought they were invincible and found they were mortal, after all.

It was a look he'd never wanted to see again—especially on the face of a woman with whom he'd been making love.

"It's the electricity, that's all. It's back on."

Sienna tore her hand from his. "Get off me."

Her voice was shaky. Okay. He could understand that it would be. The lights had spooked him, too.

"Sienna. Listen to me. It's just the power—"

"I said, get off me."

"Honey, calm down. The lights—"

"Get—off!"

Her voice was shrill. It went with the way she was looking at him, as if he were a monster instead of a man. That was another look he'd seen before. It had been in Linda's eyes the night she'd walked out.

Wordlessly, he rolled away, got to his feet. She grabbed for the discarded sweats, yanked them on and plopped down on the edge of the hearth.

"Look," he said carefully, "I know the timing was bad but—"

"Yes. It certainly was. Another couple of minutes, you'd have had what you wanted all along."

"That's a lie."

"Lock the door, you said."

"Yes." His tone was flat. "That's what I told you to do."

"What you didn't bother telling me was that you had a key."

"I didn't have a key."

"I locked the door. You opened it. What? Did you use magic?"

"Sienna—" Jesse ran his hands through his hair. "I was worried about you."

"Worried I'd steal stuff from the dresser drawers? After all, why wouldn't I? According to you, I'm here to steal artifacts from the Blackwolf Canyon ruins."

His eyes narrowed. "Stop it."

Sienna tossed her head. Despite his growing anger, he couldn't help noticing the way her soft curls flew around her flushed face. "What a pair we are. Me, a thief. And you a man who—who takes advantage of defenseless women."

"Watch yourself," he said, the words low and dangerous.

"God, how I wish it were morning!"

"My sentiments, exactly."

"There must be a way to get help." She looked up at him. "Can't you call someone?"

"I tried, remember? The phones are out."

"What about using your cell?"

"My what?"

"Or do you need a SAT way out here?"

"A SAT? A cell? What in hell are you talking about?"

"You don't know what a cell phone is?"

"I have no idea."

He could almost see the fight go out of her. She said nothing for a long moment. Then she bent her head; her hair tumbled around her face. And he knew she was weeping.

Damn it. He wanted to be angry at her, but how could he be? All his anger drained away. He fought back the desire to take her in his arms and soothe her. No way was he going to touch her again. Instead, he squatted down next to her.

"Don't cry," he said gruffly. "This was my fault."

She shook her head. "No. I shouldn't have—I'm not the kind of woman who—" She looked up. Her eyes, glittering with tears, focused on his. "I'm sorry for the things I said."

"Yeah. That makes two of us."

"It's just… I don't understand any of this. We're strangers." She took a shaky breath. "And yet, I never wanted a man the way I—the way I wanted you…."

Her honesty caught him by surprise. In his experience, women weren't usually given to accepting responsibility for their actions.

"I'm sorry if I led you on," she whispered.

Another word, he was going to say to hell with everything and gather her in his arms, and where would that get him? She'd wanted to have sex and then she'd changed her mind. The last thing he needed was another round of yes-no frustration.

Sex was only sex and he could get it elsewhere. That moment he'd thought what was happening with her was something special….

Foolishness, nothing more.

She'd barged into his life, but soon things would be on

track again. The thing was to get through what remained of the night, drive her to Bozeman and move on with his plans.

"Jesse?"

"Yeah." His tone was polite. He patted her hand, got to his feet. Whatever she was, she was more trouble than he needed, never mind the soft words of apology.

"You should have left me on that ledge."

"Trying for sympathy?"

She flinched; he knew what he'd said was unkind, but look where being kind had gotten him.

"Trying for the truth," she said as she stood up beside him. "If you'd left me there, life might have been simpler for the both of us."

He gave a brittle laugh. "Too bad you didn't tell me that this morning."

"Would you have done it, if I had?"

"Damned right," he growled, and then he sighed. "No. Hell, how could I?" His mouth twisted. "I couldn't even leave you to freeze in that bedroom a little while ago."

Her chin came up. "I would not have frozen."

He wanted to smile; he liked hearing that edge in her voice again, but what he needed was to keep things at the status quo. A little distance. No more letting his body's needs get in the way of things. "Well, I guess we'll never know."

She nodded, her chin still lifted in defiance…and then, without warning, the tears in her eyes spilled down her cheeks.

"I've been horrible," she whispered.

"No. You haven't. You're just upset and—"

"Horrible," she said again, and he forgot everything he'd just told himself about her barging into his life, about getting through the night, about sex just being sex. He forgot everything, gathered her into his arms…

And kissed her.

The kiss was gentle and soft; it transcended whatever anger still smoldered within him.

"Sienna," he said softly, and she shook her head, kept her lips against his until he framed her face with his hands. At last, he lifted his head, wincing when he saw her tear-stained eyes, the fragile skin beneath them looking as bruised as crushed lilacs. "Baby, forgive me. You were right, I took advantage of you and—"

Lightly, she lay her fingers over his mouth.

"You didn't take advantage. I told you the truth. I wanted you, too. Being in your arms made me feel safe."

"Ah. You're good for a man's ego."

He said it with absolute solemnity. She blushed. Then, as he'd hoped, she smiled. The sight made his heart lift.

"I didn't mean that the way it sounded. What I meant was—"

"You don't have to explain." Jesse wrapped his arms around her and drew her close against him. "And you're right. I'll keep you safe, I promise."

Silence. Then she spoke in a small, soft voice.

"What if you can't? What if there are some things that— that even you can't protect me from?"

She could feel the sudden tension in his body.

"You're afraid of more than the storm," he said.

She buried her face against him.

"Tell me what it is."

She shook her head.

"Is it that guy, Jack? The one who deserted you?"

What she heard in his voice frightened her. "No," she said quickly, looking up at him. "Jack's nothing. What I told you before was the truth. He doesn't mean a thing to me and he didn't desert me, I promise."

Jesse's eyes searched hers. Finally, he nodded. "Okay. Scratch Jack from the picture. Then, what are you afraid of? Tell me."

She wanted to. Carrying this incredible secret was getting harder and harder.

"Sienna?"

"I want to tell you. But—but it's too crazy…."

"Try me."

She hesitated. "You promise you won't think I've lost my mind?"

"You're asking this of a guy who paints his face and rides out to watch the summer solstice?"

That won him another smile. Amazing, how good that made him feel.

"Okay." Still, she hesitated. How did she say this? How did you tell someone you were from a different time?

"Sienna?"

"The thing is—see, the thing is, it's 2010."

His eyebrows rose. "I don't get it. Twenty-ten what?"

"The year. My year."

"Your year for what?" he said with a puzzled smile.

Sienna closed her eyes, then blinked them open. "Actually— actually, I think we should talk about this another time."

"Sienna—"

"I'm tired and confused, Jesse. All I want to do is sleep."

What he wanted were answers, but he knew now wasn't the time to get them, so he smiled and told her that was a great idea.

"You can sleep here. It's going to take time for the house to warm up, but you'll be all right by the fire. Okay?"

"What about you?"

"I'll take the bedroom."

"You'll be cold."

"Foolish woman. Indian brave no feel cold."

She laughed. Actually laughed. He flashed an answering grin when what he wanted was to pump his fist in the air.

"Okay," he said briskly, "you settle down here. I'll be right down the hall. Just call me if—"

"Don't go." The words came out on one swift breath. "Stay with me, Jesse. Please. Just hold me, that's all. Can you do that?"

Hell, no. He was a man, not a saint.

"Never mind," she said quickly. "Why would you want to? It was a crazy request. You go ahead. I'll be—"

Jesse put a finger under her chin. Tilted her face to his. Brushed his lips softly over hers. Then he knelt on the bed of blankets and offered Sienna his hand, the same way he had hours before on the sacred stone.

But it wasn't the same. This time, instead of hesitating, she put her palm against his.

He drew her down beside him. Lay back, curved his arm around her. And when she yawned softly and lay her head on his shoulder, her hand over his heart, he knew that this, just this, was somehow as meaningful as what they'd been doing before the damned lights came on.

She was asleep in seconds. No nightmares for her now, he thought as he pressed a light kiss to her hair.

And none for him.

For the first time in months, Jesse Blackwolf fell into a deep, peaceful sleep.

CHAPTER EIGHT

JESSE came awake the same way he always did, mind and body alert and ready for whatever might be waiting for him—but with one huge difference.

He'd slept straight through the night, something he hadn't done since before 'Nam. Instead of impenetrable darkness, the living room was filled with sunlight pouring from a brilliantly blue sky.

And he'd slept the night with a woman in his arms.

Not just a woman.

Sienna.

A soft, warm Sienna, still lying in his embrace, her head against his shoulder. He drew her even closer, turned his head so her silken hair brushed his chin.

It felt wonderful to have her tucked against him this way. Was she the reason he had not awakened every hour, as he'd done for so long it had started to seem normal?

No. Of course not.

That he'd slept through the night was just a quirk. Or maybe, with luck, his sleep pattern was finally starting to change. Whatever the reason, it surely didn't have a thing to do with the stranger in his arms.

Of course it didn't.

Jesse shifted his weight a little, just enough so he could get a better look at her. Amazing. He still wasn't sure why she'd turned up in the canyon yesterday, but whatever the reason, she'd had one hell of a day. And, okay, maybe he hadn't made things any easier.

Bottom line, she'd been through a lot—so how could she look so beautiful, even under the merciless glare of the morning sun?

Her hair was a cloud of gold, brown and bronze curls, her lashes a dark sweep against her cheeks. Her lips were slightly parted, her breath warm against his naked flesh.

If he angled his head a little, he could lean down and kiss those lips.

He could do more than that.

Damned right, he could.

His reaction was swift and entirely male, an erection so rock-hard it was close to painful, accompanied by a burst of images in his head, starting with him kissing her awake. Caressing her. Cupping her breasts, bringing them to his lips, looking up as her violet eyes turned deepest blue.

Jesse, she'd sigh, and this time, instead of letting his hunger take over, he'd keep himself under control.

Hey, control was his thing. Control had saved his ass in 'Nam; his men had called him the Iceman. It was what Linda had taken to calling him, too, though she hadn't meant it as a compliment.

You never let go, Jesse, she'd said, and she was probably right, he never did, but if a man let go, he might never find his way back to himself....

Jesse slid his arm from under Sienna's shoulders, folded his arms beneath his head and stared blindly at the ceiling.

Never mind all that. He'd come awake with a take-no-prisoners hard-on. End of story. It was a strictly physiological reaction to sleeping with a woman after weeks, months of celibacy.

More to the point, it was a reaction to what had gone on last night.

If he hadn't awakened that way, there'd be something wrong with him.

Definitely, it was time to do something about it.

There were a dozen women listed in his address book who'd be eager to spend a couple of hours in bed with the owner of Blackwolf Ranch. And once he put this place and its memories behind him, moved to the coast where he'd already started to make a life that suited him a lot better than this one, there'd be women lining up for the right to spend a night with him.

Any one of them would do fine, he thought coldly.

He had no romantic illusions. Not anymore. Sex was sex, not just as he'd thought last night but as he'd learned with Linda. It was purely physical. And it was a damned good thing he hadn't gone all the way with Sienna last night. Women were nothing but complications. This one had been in his life, what, twenty-four hours? Look how she'd already complicated it.

Complexity was the last thing he wanted. Things were finally right where he wanted them and that was the way he intended to keep them. Simple. Straightforward. No emotional ups and downs, no promises that inevitably turned out to be lies.

Absolutely, that was how he wanted it. He wasn't about to confuse things by getting involved with a woman who'd turned up out of nowhere, whose reasons for intruding into his life were clouded, to say the least.

Sienna's life was hers to worry over, not his.

Jesse's jaw tightened. Time to get up, get moving and, most of all, get this stranger out of his life.

She was still sleeping. Good, he thought as he got to his feet. By the time she was up, he'd have showered, made coffee, put some food in his belly. He'd have come up with a plan for how to deal with her.

Contacting the sheriff, never a real option, was definitely out.

No matter how badly he wanted her gone, a man who'd come within seconds of burying himself inside a woman would have to be out of his mind to turn her over to the law. He might be cold-hearted, as Linda had said, but he wasn't a complete SOB.

His bedroom was still cool—it would take a while for the chill of the night to wear off—but when he wrenched the shower lever all the way to hot, the water poured out just the way he liked it.

Quickly, he stripped off his clothes, dumped them in the hamper.

He'd give Sienna breakfast. Drive her into Bozeman. If the guy she insisted was her professor and not her boyfriend was there, waiting there for her, fine. If he wasn't, well, that would be fine, too. Once he got her to town, she'd be on her own. She could take a bus, a plane, rent a car, go back to wherever she'd come from.

If she needed money, he'd give her some.

Then he'd walk away.

Jesse stepped into the shower stall, turned his face up to the spray.

He'd have to put in a couple of days cleaning up the damage the storm had undoubtedly left behind. Downed trees. Broken fences. Whatever. Then he'd go through the sale documents one last time, sign them, and all this—the ranch, the canyon, the memories he no longer wanted—would be done with.

His new life was waiting.

"San Francisco," he said as he dumped shampoo on his hair, "here I come."

Yeah, he'd tried that new life once before and it hadn't worked out, but things had changed. *He* had changed. California, not Montana, was where he belonged.

He caught a glimpse of himself in the mirror over the vanity. The face, the eyes were the same. Cool. Maybe even a little empty. Maybe he hadn't changed, after all….

Jesse snorted. The hell with trying to figure it out. Worrying a thing half to death never got a man anywhere. That was what starting over was all about, wasn't it?

"Damned right," he said, and he flattened his hands against the glass of the shower wall, bent his head and let the spray beat down on his aching muscles.

Sienna heard the distant hiss of running water and decided it was safe to open her eyes.

She'd been awake forever. Since right after Jesse had awakened, anyway. One second she'd been dreaming that she was lying in the arms of a gorgeous stranger. The next, she'd realized the dream was true, she *was* lying in the arms of a gorgeous stranger. But before she could do anything about it, at least put some distance between them, she'd felt Jesse's long, powerful body shift against hers, felt the impact of his gaze on her.

And the sexy pressure of his erection.

That was when she'd decided to pretend she was still asleep.

Whatever had happened between them last night… No way could she face him this morning. It was too embarrassing….

Or maybe too tempting to just look up into those probing eyes, move against him, say his name and offer herself to him so they could finish what they'd started.

You really must be crazy, she'd told herself, and she hadn't moved a muscle. She'd faked sleep until, finally, he'd risen to his feet and walked away, his fading footsteps so determined, so obviously a message that she knew she'd done the right thing.

It was daylight, the storm was over.

And Jesse Blackwolf would be delighted to see her gone.

She felt the same way. She wanted out, the sooner the better. If she moved fast enough, she might even avoid facing him, because what did a woman say to a man after she'd been naked in his arms? After he'd touched her with hot intimacy even though they were strangers?

Sienna threw her arm over her eyes. Just remembering made her face heat. She'd never done anything like that in her life. She wasn't into hooking up with a guy for the night. She'd been with two men and she'd known both for months before things had progressed that far. And even then, she hadn't felt the way she'd felt with Jesse last night.

The liquid rush of pleasure. The shocking realization that she was, that she wanted to be, totally out of control. The desire to let a man do anything he wanted to her...

Sienna shot to her feet. She was wasting time when there was none to waste.

Surely, a house like this had a zillion bathrooms. She needed to shower away yesterday's grime. And Jesse's touch. His intimate, knowing touch.

The house had two wings. She headed for the opposite one. The very first door she tried opened onto a bedroom, and, yes, it had an attached bath. Sienna shut the bedroom door, locked it, went into the bathroom and locked that door, as well.

Not that a locked door had stopped Jesse last night.

If he came for her...

Her heart began to race. No. She wasn't going there. He

wouldn't come, and even if he did, she'd have no difficulty telling him she didn't want him.

She stripped off the sweats, let them fall to the floor. She'd have to wear them again. Her own stuff was probably still wet and mud-soaked…and who gave a damn what she wore? What mattered was getting out of here.

A bar of wrapped soap and small, unused bottles of shampoo and conditioner stood on a marble ledge. No doubt about it, this was a room for guests.

A bubble of crazed laughter rose in her throat.

Had there ever been a stranger guest than she? A 2010 guest in a 1975 world?

"Do not start on that now," she said—and thought, *Great, now she'd taken to talking to herself.* But *Herself* was right, this wasn't the time to worry over the impossibility of her situation.

After she left here? Yes. But not now.

She showered, shampooed in record time. Turned off the water. Toweled off. Ran her hands through her hair. Put on the, ugh, dirty sweats. What else? Did she owe Jesse a note? Maybe there was pen and paper in one of these drawers. Even if there were, what would she write?

Dear Mr. Blackwolf…

A little formal, all things considered.

Dear Jesse: Thank you for everything.

No good, either. She wasn't about to thank him for everything.

Okay. How about, *Hi, thanks for the sweats. I'll mail them back once I've bought something else to wear….*

Sienna stood still.

Buy clothes? With what? She had no purse. No wallet. That meant no cash, no checkbook, no charge cards, no ATM card. If she was hallucinating, that wouldn't be a problem—but she wasn't. She knew that now, even if she didn't want to think about it. Absolutely, she didn't, because if she did, she'd end up in that psycho ward.

Her hands began trembling. Hell, all of her was trembling.

She took a deep breath, but it wasn't deep, it was shaky. Still, she took another. Held it. Let it out. Did it again while her thoughts scrabbled around like laboratory mice in a cage.

Forget the note.

Just go.

But she needed a plan.

She'd start by walking to the main road. There had to be a main road, even here in the middle of nowhere. Step two, flag down a ride. Get to town. Find a branch of her bank. It was a major bank, there had to be a branch in Bozeman. In fact, she'd seen one on her way from the airport….

But that was then.

This was now. This was another time.

Who knew if the bank existed?

Don't do that, she told herself as she cracked open the bedroom door. *Don't think negatively. Think positively.* Assume the bank was there. She'd go in, tell them her stuff had been stolen, that she had an account in a branch in New York and could they arrange for a cash transfer, and yes, that sounded great except she didn't have an account at a branch in New York, not yet, she didn't have an account anywhere.

She didn't exist. She hadn't been born. She—

"Sienna?"

She blinked. Jesse stood outside the bedroom, looking so solid, so real. She wanted to fling herself into his arms. Instead, she gave him what she hoped was a there-you-are-and-thanks-for-everything smile.

"Hi."

"You okay?"

So much for the thanks-for-everything smile. Not that the question meant anything. He asked it with all the interest of a stranger on the street.

"Yes, yes, I'm fine. I was just…" She gestured behind her, toward the bathroom. "I was thinking it feels great to have showered. I hope you don't mind…?"

"No. Of course not." A brief pause. "Well—"

"Yes. Well…" Her lips felt as if the smile were stuck to them. "I, ah, I want to thank you for—"

"There's coffee."

"Coffee," she said brightly, and flashed another smile. God, she was turning into a TV commercial. "Actually, I thought— I thought I'd just—just, you know, get going…."

"Right. I figured that. Coffee, and then I'll drive you into Bozeman."

"Just point me to the highway and I'll get a lift."

"No." The determination in the single word surprised her. "I mean—" He cleared his throat. "I'll take you to town."

Of course he would. That way he'd be sure she wasn't going to turn up on his property again.

"Thank you. If you don't mind, I'd just as soon pass on the coffee. Okay?"

He nodded, then looked her over. "Sorry I don't have anything that would fit you better."

"This is fine."

"Your sneakers are probably stiff with mud—"

"They'll do."

"Good. Good." A muscle knotted in his jaw. "Look, Sienna, about last night—"

"I'm just going to get those sneakers," she said quickly, brushing past him.

She didn't get very far. His hand curled around her arm. "I was out of line."

"We already talked about this, remember? I'm as responsible for what happened as you are."

"Still, I owe you an apology."

"Fine. Apology accepted—assuming you've accepted mine."

Jesse held out his hand. She looked at it for a long moment before she took it.

"Deal," he said.

She nodded. "Deal."

He smiled. So did she. But when she looked up at him, she saw an intensity in his dark eyes that left her breathless, and saw, too, a question she could answer simply by taking a step toward him.

But she didn't. She couldn't. Because if he took her in his arms again, she would be more lost than she already was.

The handshake ended.

"I'll bring the truck around front," he said, as if the moment had not happened, and she said, "Fine," and moved past him, and knew that the sooner she got out of this place, the better.

Because of detritus from yesterday's storm, the drive took almost two hours.

Downed trees, a swollen creek, a fallen power line all required Jesse's concentration. Just as well. It gave him a reason to keep quiet after a few desultory remarks.

He had no idea what to say to the woman seated beside him.

She hadn't been big on conversation, either. In fact, she'd only made one remark since getting into his Chevy Silverado. She'd looked at his eight-track tape player and given a choked laugh.

"Something funny?"

"No. No, not at all. It's just…that's an eight-track, right?"

His brows lifted. "What else would it be?"

An iPod, she thought giddily, and fought back a sense of rising hysteria.

"Want to hear something?"

She nodded.

"Pick whatever you like," he said, jerking his head toward the box of tapes on the floor near her feet.

"The Eagles," she said, with that little laugh again, as if she'd stumbled across something completely unexpected. "Oh, I love their music! You, too?"

"Yeah," he'd said. "They're okay."

The truth was, they were his favorite band, but admitting that seemed to be admitting too much.

Now, as they approached the center of town, "One of These Nights" playing softly in the background, Jesse cleared his throat.

"There's a hotel on Main Street that's not too bad."

Sienna swung toward him. She knew he'd said something, but her brain seemed to have stopped working.

"What?"

He reached out, silenced the tape player.

"I said, there's a hotel on Main that's passable."

She nodded. It wasn't the music that had kept her from hearing him, it was the realization that this place, this town, was not the one she'd flown into a couple of days ago. Some of the buildings were the same, but if this was Main Street, where were those staples of American life that had been here then?

Arby's. Taco Bell. Burger King. They were gone. Or they'd never been. Either way, she was lost, lost, lost—

"Unless you and the boyfriend already have a room."

"For the last time, there is no boyfriend. We don't have a room. *I* don't have a room. We were camping in the canyon—"

"My canyon."

She opened her mouth, closed it again. Looked straight ahead, not at him.

"Just let me out anywhere you want."

"You pick it. The airport? Someplace that'll rent you a car? The Greyhound terminal?"

"Greyhound? Oh. The bus station. Yes, that's fine."

Jesse nodded, The terminal was dead ahead. He pulled to the curb and stopped. He hadn't meant to bark at her about the damned canyon or to toss yet another accusation about Jack. Who cared if she'd been in his canyon? And she'd already said Jack was her professor, and he believed her.

It was just that he was in one miserable mood. No reason for it. Actually, he should have been feeling great, getting rid of an unwanted encumbrance.

"You want me to wait while you go in and check the schedule?"

"No," she said quickly. "No, thank you. I—I'll be fine."

"Do you need money?"

"No," she said again.

Still, he reached in his pocket, took out some bills and held them toward her. "Go ahead. Just in case."

She looked at him and knew she'd sooner starve than take anything more from him.

"I don't need it."

Jesse shrugged, opened his door, stepped down from the truck and went around to her side. She had already opened her door and stepped onto the sidewalk.

"Well," he said.

Sienna flashed a bright smile. "Thanks for everything," she said, even though she'd promised herself she wouldn't.

The muscle in his jaw locked and unlocked. "Damn it, Sienna," he said roughly, but before he could say more, she turned and ran into the bus station. The door shut after her.

Jesse stood, unmoving.

She was gone.

It was a relief. It was what he'd wanted, wasn't it? To get her out of his life?

Maybe he should have asked her where she'd go. Or how she'd get there. She'd said she didn't need money, but she didn't have a purse. Her clothes were still on the floor in his house. If she'd had a wallet, he sure as hell hadn't seen it.

All he'd seen was sadness in her eyes, and fear—and then, this morning, there'd been more, something that had made him ache to take her in his arms and tell her not to leave, never to leave, which was exactly what he'd come within a heartbeat of saying….

A bus pulled out into the road. Was she on it? She couldn't be. She'd only just gone through those doors….

"Sienna?"

He started toward the terminal, slowly at first, then faster and faster so that by the time he reached it, he was running. He flung the door open, stood still, looked around him.

The waiting room was empty.

"Sienna!" A worn-out-looking guy dozing on a bench jerked awake. "Sienna," Jesse shouted…and, suddenly, he saw her, standing at the far end of the gloomy room, looking fragile and lost.

"Jesse?"

Her face lit. It made his heart turn over. He had never thought a woman would look at him that way again, as if he were all she'd ever wanted or needed, and he'd damned well never imagined he'd want a woman to look at him like that, either.

Now he knew he'd never wanted it, or wanted one particular woman, half this much.

He wanted to open his arms and gather her in, tell her what he felt…but a man only made a fool of himself over a woman one time and he had met his quota.

So he strode toward her instead, stopped inches away and put his hands on his hips.

"Where are you going?"

The glow in her eyes dimmed so fast he thought maybe he'd imagined it.

"Excuse me?"

"I said, where are you going? Why didn't you take that money? Aren't you even going to try to find this guy, Jack? He brought you here, didn't he? Shouldn't he be looking for you?"

"That's five questions," she said, lifting her chin. "And not one of them is any of your business."

That muscle that knotted in his jaw whenever he was ticked off was going full speed. What had made him come after her? Not concern or caring, that was certain, though it was what she'd foolishly thought when she first saw him.

She knew why he'd come after her. The same thing that had made him risk his neck getting her off that ledge, that had made him give her shelter, food, even these ridiculous sweats.

He was a man of honor. He felt responsible for her, but then, he'd probably feel that same responsibility for anybody. It had nothing to do with her.

Somehow, stupid as it seemed, that was infuriating.

"I am not your responsibility," she said coldly. "You got that, Mr. Blackwolf?"

Jesse's eyes narrowed. He glared at her, glared some more.

Then he said something in what she figured might have been Sioux or Comanche, took her none-too-gently by the arm and, despite her yelps of protest, marched her out of the terminal and back to the Silverado.

CHAPTER NINE

SHE fought all the way, digging in her heels, calling him names he hadn't thought women knew, but then, this was a woman like none he'd ever met. Tough. Strong. Fragile. Vulnerable. She was a mass of contradictions and, damn it, so was he, or else why would he have yanked her out of that gloomy bus station and hustled her back into the cab of his truck?

"Do not try to get away," he said grimly, once he got her there, "because I'll just go after you again and bring you back. You got that?"

The look she gave him said she got it, and more. Despite everything, he came close to laughing. What mattered was that he didn't, he just went around the truck, got into the driver's seat, turned the key, jammed his foot to the floor and the Silverado skidded onto the road, the roar of its engine and the squeal of its tires a good approximation of the anger boiling inside him.

Yes, but who was he angry at? Her? Or him?

He drove fast, up Main Street, out of town, turned off on a muddy excuse for a road he remembered from his high school days, a place where you could cut classes and find half a dozen other bored jerks doing the same thing. Once there, he shut off the engine and looked at her.

"Question one. Where did you figure on going?"

Nothing. She went on staring straight ahead, arms folded, profile looking as if it had been done by a chisel.

"Okay, question two. How were you going to get there? Far as I can tell, you don't have a dime to your name."

Still nothing. Jesse glowered.

"Question three. Why didn't you want to go looking for Jack the Quitter?"

Was that a faint twitch of her mouth? Maybe they were making progress.

"If I were in your shoes, all alone, no money, nothing but my clothes on my back—"

"Your clothes," she said caustically. "My back, your clothes. Don't you want to point that out, too?"

"If I were in your shoes," he said, as if she hadn't interrupted him, "I'd sure as hell want to locate Jack the Jerk."

Another twitch. "Very amusing."

"Very valid, you mean. Why aren't you interested in finding him? The man brought you here. He left you in the canyon. He's responsible for you."

She swung toward him. "Look, take my word on this. Jack isn't—he isn't here." She turned away, fixed her eyes on the windshield again. "Now, will you take me back to the bus station?"

"You haven't answered my other questions. Where are you going to go?"

"Wherever the first bus out will take me."

"And how will you pay for a ticket?" More stony silence. Jesse grabbed her shoulders and turned her toward him. "Damn it, woman, stop pretending I'm a stranger. I saw you dressed." His eyes narrowed. "I saw you undressed. Damned near every inch of you, and—"

"Such a gentleman," she said, her defiance matched by the rise of color in her face.

"I'm not a gentleman. I never pretended I was."

"I don't think you could. Pretend to be a gentleman, I mean. A man like you just—just takes what he wants and to hell with—"

She gasped as he pulled her against him and kissed her, his mouth hard and bruising against hers.

"Stop while you're still ahead," he growled when he lifted his head. "If I'd taken what I wanted last night, things would be a lot different this morning."

"I don't know what that's supposed to mean," she said, her voice trembling.

He didn't know what it was supposed to mean, either. If they'd made love, it wouldn't have made a bit of difference. Morning still would have come and he'd still have sent her on her way….

Except, he *hadn't* sent her on her way, even though they hadn't made love.

Just as he'd figured, she was complicating his life and he seemed powerless to stop it.

He let go of her, sat back, clasped the steering wheel and stared out the windshield.

"Okay. You're broke. You have nowhere to go. Nobody you can turn to for help." He looked at her, his voice cold. "Have I left anything out?"

Sienna lifted her shoulders, then dropped them in what he assumed was meant as a what-else-is-new gesture. It made him want to tug her into his arms again and kiss her not as he just had, with anger at himself, at her, at fate, but with tenderness.

He wouldn't, of course.

Why should he feel tender toward a woman who'd dropped into his life without invitation?

Still, no way could he simply abandon her. Pretending otherwise had been foolish. His mother had always teased him about bringing home strays. Dogs, cats, one time an orphaned raccoon, another a baby possum. Linda hadn't teased him about it so much as she'd chastised him for it. She had enough to do, dealing with him, she'd say; the last thing she needed was a stray underfoot.

But Linda had nothing to do with this. This was about Sienna. She was a problem, and until he figured out what to do about it, he'd handle it.

He took the bills he'd tried to give her earlier from his shirt pocket, sat forward, took his wallet from his jeans, thumbed out all the bills and held all the money toward her. She looked at his hand, then at him. The expression on her face would have frozen an entire ocean.

"I already told you. No."

"What do you mean, no?"

"I mean, no. En-Oh. No. I don't want anything from you except a lift back to the bus station."

He stared at her for a long minute. Then he shook his head, stuffed the bills and the wallet into his pocket.

"You," he said grimly, "are impossible."

Sienna thought that he might be right. But she didn't want his money, didn't want him thinking he could buy her off, didn't want anything except what he had not offered, and, God, she wasn't just impossible, she was crazy.

She was furious with him, and he hadn't done anything but show her another act of kindness even if he'd done it with all the charm of a grizzly.

Even if it wasn't the one thing she really wanted.

When he'd come through the door at the bus station, calling her name; when he'd located her and come toward her… Her heart, her foolish, foolish heart, had bounced straight into her throat.

He'd come for her, she'd thought. This time, he really had come for her. He didn't want to let her leave him. He was going to tell her that, to say it didn't matter how or when or where they'd stumbled across each other, all that counted was that they had.

But he hadn't done or said anything remotely like that. Instead, he'd grabbed her as if she were a—a sack of laundry, hauled her to his truck, driven her out here in grim silence and then asked her questions she couldn't answer.

The worst of it was, she couldn't blame him.

They were nothing to each other. She'd romanticized everything. The storm, the kisses, the sexual heat they'd generated, and now she was taking out her anger on him.

"Okay," he said, and slapped his palms against the steering wheel. "Okay. You won't accept a handout. How about a job, instead?"

A job. Yes. That sounded reasonable. She could accumulate a little money, take the time to determine what to do next.

She turned toward him.

"Do you know someone with a job to fill?"

He shrugged those broad shoulders. "Maybe."

Maybe. The man was a wellspring of information.

"Doing what?"

He glanced at her. "Does it matter?"

No, it didn't. She'd take whatever she could get.

"Yes," she said, lying through her teeth. "A person likes to know what she's applying for before she applies."

Brilliant. He raised his eyebrows. She fought against raising hers.

"Well," he said thoughtfully, "what can you do? There must be something besides anthropology."

He made the profession sound like a disease. Sienna sat a little straighter.

"I studied business for two years before switching majors."

He nodded, obviously not impressed. "So, you can type?"

That did it. She swung toward him again, this time breathing fire.

"If you mean, can I do word processing…"

"I mean, can you type? Whatever 'word processing' is, it doesn't interest me."

No. It wouldn't. She was thirty-five-plus years ahead of him in technology and light-years ahead in gender equality, but the old saying was accurate. Beggars couldn't be choosers, and if ever there'd been a beggar, it was she.

"Yes," she said. "I can type."

He nodded again. "There's a job opening for a typist. Well, a secretary."

"A personal assistant," she said sweetly, because she couldn't help herself.

He snorted. "This is not a job that involves arranging flowers or planning parties. It's for a woman who can do some typing. Some shorthand. Brew coffee, run errands, you know the routine."

She certainly did. When she'd studied business, older women in the department had talked about the days when men automatically assumed those functions were strictly sex-related. But she could survive stereotyping for a few weeks, because, surely, it wouldn't take longer than that to get her head around what had happened, save a little money and plan a way out.

"Can you do those things?"

"I don't take shorthand." Did anyone, in her world? "But I can handle the rest of it."

"Fine."

He turned the key. The Silverado gave a sexy growl and he shifted into Reverse, laid his arm over the seat back, peered behind them and began backing toward the main road. His hand brushed her shoulder; an electric tingle sizzled through her. She caught her breath. The sooner she got this job, got a room in town, got away from Jesse Blackwolf, the better.

Say something, she told herself, say something about the job, about the world, just say something that takes your mind off him.

"Where's this job located?"

"Outside town."

Outside town. How would she get back and forth to work? She wasn't going to ask.

"What's it pay?"

He glanced at her, then at the road. "Enough."

"Enough? Enough?" Sienna glared at him. "What's that mean? I'll have to find a room, buy food, buy clothes...."

"One-twenty a week."

The amount was surely a joke—or was that what a secretary was expected to live on in the seventies?

Sienna lifted her chin. "No way."

"One-thirty. Plus room and board."

"You mean, I'm going to live where I work?"

"Yeah." His tone turned sarcastic. "Unless you'd prefer to drive there in the car you don't own."

"Very amusing." She folded her arms. "What kind of business is it?"

Jesse shrugged. "A little of this, a little of that. Ranching, mostly, with some other stuff tossed in."

Was she paranoid along with everything else, or was he being evasive? "What other stuff?"

"Jeez." He huffed out a breath as he tapped his horn and cut around a truck towing a horse trailer. "Stuff. Finance."

"Excel, you mean?"

That won her another glance. "I don't know if you'd call this guy one who excels at finance, but he's done okay."

"No. I didn't mean does he excel at it, I meant does he use Ex…" She sighed. "Never mind."

"So, you can handle the numbers part? Keep a ledger?"

Not without a computer and software, but why tell him that?

"I'm good at on-the-job learning," she said airily. "What's my boss's name?"

"His name is Jesse Blackwolf," Jesse said, and made a sharp right through the gate that led onto Blackwolf Ranch.

"What?" Sienna sat up straight. "Forget it! I am not living here, sleeping here, working here—working for you."

"You got any better ideas, I'm ready to hear them."

"I want a job in town."

"Sure." He gave a lazy, infuriating laugh. "Only one little problem, baby. There are no jobs in town."

"Don't call me 'baby.' And there must be jobs. Small towns always need waitstaff."

"Waitstaff," he said, and chuckled. "You mean waiters and waitresses? Well, yes. But Bozeman gets more than its share of skiers, hikers, whatever. They take those jobs faster than you can say 'Thank you, Jesse, for finding me a job.' If you were ever going to say 'thanks,' that is."

"I… You…" She sank her teeth into her bottom lip. He was right. She was lucky he was willing to hire her. All she'd have to do was make sure he knew it was a business arrangement.

She told him that, in precisely those words, as he pulled up in front of the house.

"This is strictly business," she said coldly, "and don't you forget it."

She was out of the truck before he could say anything. He thought about going after her as she flounced toward the porch, of taking her in his arms and showing her that what was between them was business, all right. Unfinished business.

But she was right.

He'd keep his distance. She'd keep hers. It was a big ranch. And he actually did need a secretary, assuming she was competent, someone who could type his letters, sort his mail, keep the ranch's books so his accountants wouldn't scratch their heads and give him lectures at the end of every quarter when they came by....

Hell.

He wasn't going to be here another quarter. He was selling this place; why had he forgotten that? She'd be out of a job in another couple of days....

"Jesse?"

He swung around as he stepped from the cab. His foreman was trotting toward him. He'd given Chuck and the rest of his men the weekend off. He'd wanted to be alone so he could figure out how to tell them he was selling the ranch, that there'd be no more work for them, and, instead, he'd spent his time first chasing after spiritual hocus-pocus and then after a woman.

A woman.

He was a fool, he thought grimly. Worse than a fool. He'd wasted precious time instead of dealing with reality.

"Chuck. I'm glad to see you. We need to talk."

"Yeah. I saw the damage in the southeast pasture. I've

got a couple of men out there already, fixing those fence posts, but—"

"No. Not about that. I meant…" Jesse looked toward the front door just as Sienna opened it. He frowned and ran his hand through his hair. "Give me a half hour, then come to the office, okay?"

His foreman looked at Sienna's receding back, then at him. "Sure," he said, and headed for the barn.

Jesse stepped inside the quiet house. "Sienna?"

"I'm here," she said.

His eyebrows lifted. She'd found the office without him; she was seated behind his big desk, a stack of papers before her. Not the ranch-sale documents, he saw with relief. They were untouched, safe inside a file folder. What Sienna had in front of her was his mail, all of it. It had been accumulating since his last secretary had quit a couple of weeks ago.

She'd said he had the disposition of a rabid skunk.

Maybe not a skunk, he'd thought, but yeah, okay, the rabid part fit.

Mrs. Marx had worked at a small desk in the corner of the big office. Not Sienna. She'd settled in his chair, at his desk. It dwarfed her. Even the windows behind her seemed determined to do their part. Add in that she was wearing those ridiculous oversized sweats and she should have looked silly…

She didn't.

She looked spectacular.

The sun, streaming through the glass, touched her with gold. She was frowning as she studied the paper in her hands, but he knew, when she looked up, her eyes would be that deep violet….

Violet, and filled with disdain. He saw that, too.

"Do you ever even open your mail?"

Damn, he could feel color rise in his face. "Of course."

"And your bills. Do you pay them or do you just save them until you have enough to paper a wall?"

His mouth became a hard, thin line. "I did not ask you to critique my management style, Cummings."

She snorted. "Is that what you call it? Trust me, Mr. Black-wolf. You don't need a secretary, you need a bulldozer."

"Look, I haven't had the chance to get to this stuff lately, okay? And it isn't going to matter. That's what I have to tell you about this job. See—"

"You had a couple of phone calls. I took the messages. Didn't you ever hear of voice mail?"

Jesse sighed. "I have no idea what—"

"An answering machine. You need one."

"I have one. The storm must have—"

"The call was from a Mr. Henley."

Jesse cocked his head. "Henley? What did he say?"

"Something about the investment you're interested in. He said the company might be up for grabs." Sienna glanced at a small piece of paper. "'Up for grabs.' Those were his exact words. And he said, if you're interested, you'd better be in San Francisco by late afternoon." She looked at him. "San Francisco?"

Jesse clasped his hands behind his back and paced from one side of the room to the other. In what he thought of as his other life, he'd put a bid on the controlling shares in a start-up, a small company working in the new field of computer technology. He wanted it; he knew it had one hell of a future even if he still didn't quite understand what it could do.

"And you had a call from a Mr. Harper. Something about the bill of sale for Blackwolf Ranch…?"

Damn it, this was the last thing he wanted. The two most important deals in his life, coming together at one time….

"Jesse?" Sienna's voice dropped. "You aren't really going to sell it, are you? The ranch? The canyon? All those ancient, beautiful sites?"

He swung toward her. "I'm going to do exactly what I have to do," he said coldly.

"But—"

"There's an address book in the top right-hand drawer. On the first page, you'll see phone numbers for my pilot—"

"Your what?"

"My pilot."

"You have a pilot? And a plane?"

He almost laughed. For once, the tables were turned. *He* was surprising *her*.

"The two usually go together, yes. So, call him. His name is Tony. Tell him to be ready to leave in an hour. Then find the number for a woman named Hilda."

"Listen, pal, you want to call some woman, do it your—"

"My San Francisco housekeeper," he said, and wondered why watching her bristle with resentment should have pleased him. "Tell her I'm flying in today."

"Your San Francisco housekeeper?"

"Yeah. I have a place there."

"In San Francisco," she said, a little weakly.

That pleased him, too.

He eyed her with dispassion. "As for what you're wearing…it will have to do until we get to the West Coast."

"Until *we*…" Sienna stood up. "I am not going with you."

"You want this job or not?"

"That's not the point."

Jesse lifted his eyebrows. "What is?"

What? she thought. What, indeed? How about the point was that she had no idea what was going on here? Jesse Blackwolf, he of the painted face and eagle-talon amulet, was turning into someone else. When she looked him up on Google, the ranch, the canyon, the sacred stone, there'd been nothing about—

"Answer the question. If wanting the job isn't the point, what is?"

Sienna swallowed hard. "Being your secretary is one thing. Going with you to San Francisco is—"

"—is part of the job," he said, finishing her protest with cold authority.

"You can get someone in San Francisco. Hire a temp."

She was right, he could. He'd done it before. In fact, it was what he always did on his trips to the coast. He sure as hell had never taken Mrs. Marx or any of her predecessors with him. Why would he? He had a house on Russian Hill; he'd converted one room to an office, and, really, it was all he needed. On those few occasions he'd required someone to take dictation or type a letter, he called an office temps firm.

But why go through that when he already had a secretary right here? That was the only reason for taking Sienna with him.

Of course it was. And he told her so.

"Make up your mind," he said. "Do you want this job or do you intend to quit on your first day?"

"I'm not quitting. It's just that—that—"

She stared at him. He was right; she knew that. She'd agreed to take the position. Why was she trying so hard to avoid going with him?

Was it because she knew her secretarial skills were lacking?

Or was it because things were moving too fast? Because the ground was shifting under her feet so quickly that there were times she honestly felt dizzy?

Or was it simpler than that?

Was it because, despite how she'd been sniping at Jesse, she had only to look at him and her heartbeat quickened? She couldn't stop remembering the feel of his arms, the taste of his mouth, the exquisite pleasure of his touch.

She could not feel that way about a man who didn't exist! Or a man who didn't exist when she existed! Oh, God, she had to figure this out, figure out what would happen next—

Sienna shot to her feet. "I'm not going with you," she said, rushing the words together. "You don't really need me there."

"Don't tell me what I need and don't need," he said in a low, dangerous voice.

She cried out as he scooped her into his arms, threaded a hand through her hair, brought her face to his and captured her mouth.

He kissed her hard and deep, and maybe she could have dealt with that but then his kiss changed. He kissed her slowly, with tenderness, with longing, and just as she felt as if her bones might melt, he clasped her shoulders and put her from him.

"Make those calls," he said.

And then he was gone.

CHAPTER TEN

WHO was Jesse Blackwolf, anyway?

First he kissed her until she couldn't think.

Then he walked away.

He rode horses, drove a truck, painted his face with a warrior's stripes, wore an eagle amulet—and lived in a magnificent house in the middle of a gorgeous wilderness, owned a private plane and, so he said, a home in one of the world's most sophisticated cities.

Complex didn't come close to describing him. *Surprising* might be a better word, and maybe the most surprising thing was that he thought he could take her in his arms and kiss her to silence or, at least, to acquiescence.

Thought he could? The truth was, he'd done it. Several times. And if he could pull that off so easily, was it his fault…or hers?

Never mind.

His address book was right where he'd said it would be. Sienna found the phone numbers, made the calls he'd requested. Demanded, was more like it. He had an aura of command, an I-always-get-what-I-want sensibility. Was it his military background? Was it because he was a man of the 1970s? Or was it just him?

Never mind trying to figure that out, either. Not now, anyway. She had never needed a job as badly as she needed this one.

Neither his pilot nor his housekeeper seemed surprised to hear a woman's voice relaying his instructions. Were they well trained in taking calls from a prior secretary or were they accustomed to their boss having a woman in his life? His private life. Not that she was a woman. Well, she was, of course, but she was his employee, that was all, and if he thought he could get her into his bed by taking her with him…

Sienna laughed.

If he'd wanted to take her to bed, he'd do it here. No need to fly her, what, eight, nine hundred miles? They both knew he could seduce her without half trying.

But she wasn't going to let it happen.

She was in enough of a mess. Sleeping with him would only make things worse. The last thing she needed was to connect with a complex man. A mysterious man. Google had given her hardly any information about him. She'd found that curious.

Now, knowing him, she found it credible.

An empty leather briefcase lay on a small worktable. She grabbed it, tucked a steno pad into it—good grief, a steno pad!—along with some pens and pencils.

The Internet had given her information about the canyon, the sacred stone, the tribes who'd lived on Blackwolf land a couple of hundred years ago and the people who'd inhabited it thousands of years before that. All she'd found about Jesse was his date of birth and the notation that he was "reclusive." Wikipedia had been more direct and referred to him as a loner who'd inherited the ranch on the deaths of his parents, lived on it for a few years and then…

Then, nothing.

"Sienna? Are you ready?"

She looked up, saw him in the doorway. He'd changed into close-fitting, faded jeans and a black turtleneck sweater, a tweedy light gray sport coat and what surely were hand-tooled black leather boots.

He looked as if he'd just stepped out of *GQ*.

She looked as if she'd just stepped out of a thrift shop.

And he was so beautiful he made her ache.

His plane was a Learjet.

It said so on the tail.

You could take what she knew about planes, stuff it into a walnut and have room to spare, but you didn't have to know planes to know this one was a reflection of its owner, a sleek, magnificent combination of power and purpose.

The pilot, Tony, was a man of few words. He greeted Jesse with a salute that Jesse ignored.

"Lieutenant," Tony said.

"Tony. We good to go?"

Tony nodded. "Absolutely." He gave her a sidelong glance and a polite smile.

"This is Sienna Cummings. My new secretary."

"His administrative assistant," Sienna said.

Tony's eyebrows rose, rose again when she stuck out her hand. He looked at it as if he'd never before seen a woman's hand extended that way, but after a second, he got the message and shook it.

Yet another little reminder that this was the seventies.

"You want to take the controls, Lieutenant?"

Jesse said no, not this time; he had work to do. Tony nodded; nodding seemed to be his favored form of communication. Another quick salute and he vanished into the cockpit.

Sienna looked at Jesse. "Lieutenant?"

He shrugged. "We were in the service together."

"And you know how to fly?"

A quick, cold smile. "Surprised?"

"No, not really. You just never said—"

Her tone—not just surprised but disbelieving—might have made him laugh if he hadn't grown accustomed to that kind of reaction. All his life, people had tried to fit what they knew of him into neat little boxes.

The Blackwolf kid, hell-bent on trouble. The scholarship student with the brilliant SAT scores who didn't seem to give a damn about his grades. The army recruit who could shoot the eye out of a gnat, take down a man in hand-to-hand combat without breaking a sweat—and read Schopenhauer in his spare time.

This time around, though, he'd surprised himself, first by riding out to watch the solstice before he turned his back on the nonsensical superstitions of ancestors.

And then by bringing Sienna into his life.

Who was she, really? What had brought her here? There was something she wasn't telling him. Not that he cared. Sienna Cummings was just a temporary distraction and, damn it, why hadn't he left her at the Greyhound terminal? Why had he offered her a job he didn't need filled? Better still, why had he brought her with him on this trip?

You know why, a mocking voice inside him said. *Just take her to bed and get it over with, then she'll be out of your system.*

He looked at Sienna, that surprised *"Lieutenant?"* still buzzing in his head.

"Sienna." She turned toward him. "To answer your question," he said coolly, "yes, I held the rank of lieutenant. And just to get it out of the way, yes, those were medals you saw on my uniform, including the Distinguished Service Cross. And yes, I know how to fly. I know how to do a lot of things, including not bothering with small talk. Am I being clear? Because, just in case you thought otherwise, work is the sole reason I brought you along."

Her face turned pink. Her eyes flashed. She turned to the window but he saw her hands knot together in her lap.

You are a gold-plated bastard, Blackwolf, he told himself. And a very bad liar.

He'd brought her with him because he wanted her near him. The sound of her laughter, the look of her, the way she stood up to him every time…

He wanted to get out of his seat, go to her and take her in his arms.

Instead, he dug in his pocket for a pen and a small, leather-bound notebook, opened it and began scribbling notes. That the notes were meaningless didn't matter.

Keeping busy was everything.

The flight was smooth and took less than four hours.

Sienna had never been to San Francisco before, which meant she had no way of knowing if the skyline had changed much between Jesse's day and hers. But the taxi ride from the airport had been a revelation. The city was big and busy, its roads crowded with old cars…except they weren't old. Not really. And the way people were dressed, all those silly bell-bottom trousers and platform shoes…

It might have been amusing, but it wasn't. It was, instead, a reminder—as if she needed one—that she had somehow slipped through time.

Don't think about that, she told herself, *don't!* Instead, she took refuge in a cool cynicism, as if what awaited her here was nothing out of the ordinary, starting with the moment the taxi pulled up before a glass-and-concrete tower on Russian Hill.

It was, she knew, some of the priciest real estate in the world.

She focused on keeping her face free of expression as they rode a private elevator to the penthouse floor, which turned out to be all Jesse's. Huge rooms, high ceilings, acres of glass with views of the city in all directions, including the glorious Golden Gate Bridge.

His housekeeper had left a note. It was polite and brief. The refrigerator was fully stocked, there was a stir-fry of shrimp, bok choy and snow peas ready for heating. The bedrooms were all freshly made up, the bathrooms fully stocked with Mr. Blackwolf's favorite supplies, though she advised against using the fourth bathroom because the tile work around the tub had not yet been completed.

Sienna looked up, an eyebrow raised. "The fourth bathroom? How many are there?"

"The four," Jesse said with a gruffness that was either careless or embarrassed. She couldn't be sure which. "And a half," he added, and now there was no question about it, he was embarrassed. "I wanted the place for the view."

"The view from the half bath?" she said sweetly.

"The apartment," he said with a glare—and then, to her surprise, he laughed. "It's kind of big, I admit."

Big? It was almost the size of his house. Not that she cared one way or another. It was just that this was a long way from horses and canyons and Chevy trucks. *How?* she wanted to ask. Better still, why?

But she wasn't about to ask him anything….

"Stocks," he said brusquely. "I'm an investor. A trader."

So much for cool cynicism. "Oh," she said, and he laughed

gain, this time a real laugh, straight from his belly. His flat, ard belly...

"What? Can't you think of me as an investor?"

Sienna swallowed dryly. What she'd been thinking about im didn't have a thing to do with investments, and she was ot going there! She raised her chin, gave him her best "Who ares?" look.

"Frankly, I wasn't thinking of you at all. I was thinking vhich of those four-and-a-half bathrooms would be mine."

"Pick a bedroom. They all come with bathrooms." His nouth twitched. "Though you might want to avoid the one vith the unfinished tile work."

"The only bedroom I want to avoid is the one that be-ongs to you."

She'd meant it as a cool statement of fact and saw, imme-iately, that Jesse had taken it as a challenge.

"Trust me, baby," he said softly. "If I wanted you in my edroom, you'd be there."

She felt her face heat, knew she needed a flippant rejoinder, ut her mind was blank so she made do with marching out of he room. She hadn't gotten far when he called her name.

"Sienna?"

She stopped, but she didn't turn around. "What now?"

"I have a meeting in two hours. It's business, which means ou have a meeting, too."

She swung toward him. "A meeting? I really don't want o go to a—"

"I want you ready to go in an hour and a half."

She looked down at herself. There wasn't much to get ready. Ier sweats—*his* sweats—had not magically become better-itting, and now they bore almost two days' worth of grime.

His gaze followed hers. He looked up, arms folded, one

booted foot tapping against the marble floor. "You can't go to a business meeting looking like that."

"No." She smiled, the skirmish won. "I can't. So go to your meeting, have a great time, and—"

He said something under his breath, something she didn' understand and probably was better off not understanding, and he hurried to where she stood, grabbed her arm and hustled her out the door.

A while ago, she'd have said nothing this man could do would surprise her anymore.

Taking her to Neiman Marcus blew that conviction ou of the water.

"May I help you, sir?"

If the sight of a gorgeous man propelling forward a woman wearing oversized soiled sweats was unusual, you'd never have known it from the sales clerk's polite smile.

"The lady needs something to wear," Jesse said grimly.

"Certainly, sir. Of what type?"

"Of what…" Jesse scowled. "Something appropriate for a business meeting. And fast." The clerk's eyebrows rose and Jesse took a deep breath. "Please," he said, and smiled, and damn the man, the smile—sexy, open, charming—made the clerk melt.

She hustled Sienna into a dressing room, looked her over as if she were a chicken waiting to be put into a pot.

"I'm a size eight," Sienna said, "and I like earth tones."

Might as well talk to the wall.

"A six," the woman said, "pinks and blues." And she left

Five minutes later, Sienna put the sweats back on, pushed past the sputtering clerk and out of the dressing room. Jesse was seated in a gilt chair. Someone had brought him coffee and a stack of magazines. He looked big and masculine, completely out of place and uncomfortable, which was, at least, some reason for rejoicing.

"Jesse," Sienna hissed. He looked up. "We need to find a different store. I can't afford anything here."

"No," he said, "you can't. But I can."

"I cannot permit you to—"

"This is a business expense."

"It most certainly is not!"

"And you know that because…?"

"I told you." She folded her arms. "I took business courses. Intro to Financial Accounting. Clothing is not—"

"Intro to Accounting?" His smile was pitying. "Just choose something to wear, Cummings. And leave financial decisions to someone who knows how to make them."

She couldn't come up with an answer that didn't involve four-letter words. After a moment of icy silence, he looked at his watch, then at her. "Ten minutes. I suggest you get moving."

Back to the fitting room. Five more minutes went by. He heard female voices and then Sienna was standing in front of him again.

"I cannot possibly go to a business meeting in this!"

Jesse looked her over. She had on a pink sweater with some kind of narrow bands down the front. It was tucked into purple trousers that looked as if they'd started out okay before flaring wide enough to hide a couple of dozen dwarfs in each leg. Topping it all was a long purple jacket with a collar big enough to threaten the wearer with decapitation.

Jesse tried not to laugh. A good plan, because Sienna's expression was grim.

"Madam wishes for close-fitting trousers," the clerk said with distaste. "In white, with a white silk shirt."

"And a black blazer. Calvin Klein. Or DKNY—"

The clerk sniffed. "I've never heard of those brands."

Sienna swung toward her. "No," she snapped, "I'll bet you—"

"A dress," he said calmly. "Something in deep gold or coffee-colored silk, knee length, simple and fitted."

"Surely such colors are not in vogue, sir."

"Surely such colors will complement the lady's hair. And she'll need—what did she call it? A blazer. Tan."

The clerk was back to smiling. "You mean, beige, sir."

He shrugged. "Whatever. Shoes. A handbag. The works. Just make it quick. We're running out of time."

Sienna, stuck somewhere back in Jesse's comment about wanting her in colors to complement her hair, lifted her chin.

"I make my own choices."

Jesse raised one dark eyebrows. "And I make the decisions."

If looks could kill, he would have been dead.

Sienna left the fitting room for the last time fifteen minutes later.

She was wearing a fitted jacket over a chocolate-brown silk dress, and, yes, the colors were perfect with her hair. Another swift-moving clerk had brought shoes—Jesse had bitten his lip at the sound of Sienna's laughter over whatever had been the first pair offered. This pair was fine. They were slender high heels the color of the jacket, matched by a small purse that hung from her shoulder. Someone from one of the fancy makeup counters on the first floor had popped in with a bag of tricks: lipstick, mascara, the whisk of a comb through those gold-tinged curls...

"Madam looks exquisite," the clerk said, though grudgingly.

Jesse said nothing.

"Well?" Sienna said. "Will I do?"

"You'll do," he said, and just for an instant, the air between them took on that electric heat they'd generated before. He liked what he saw, she thought, and despite all her promises to herself about not wanting him, a tremor went through her, so intense and so swift that it made her heart gallop.

Their eyes met. Time seemed to stop. Then he cleared his throat, went back to looking removed and irritated, and stood up.

"The bill," he snapped. The clerk handed it over, Jesse dealt with it, and then they went down the escalator, into another taxi, and were quickly deposited outside an imposing brick building.

"Where are we?" Sienna hissed as Jesse clamped his hand around her elbow.

"We're meeting with my financial consultant," he said, and after that, the entire day went to hell.

It was all her doing, she knew it.

And knew that her job had gone the same way.

But, really, was it entirely her fault? Didn't some of the blame start with the groomed-to-within-an-inch-of-her-life receptionist, wearing flared trousers that put her waistline in the vicinity of her ribs and, yes, shoes with what looked like a four-inch platform? The woman beamed at Jesse.

"Mr. Blackwolf, how lovely to see you, sir. Mr. Henley's expecting you."

Not even a glance spared for Sienna. Jesse didn't mention her presence, either. Okay. She was a secretary. Not a PA or an Admin Assistant. Basically, she was a PNN. *Persona non noticeable.* Or something like that.

Henley's secretary came out to greet them. "Mr. Blackwolf, sir. It's good to see you."

This time, a glance went in Sienna's direction. Sienna smiled pleasantly. "How do you do? I'm—"

"This way, Mr. Blackwolf."

Sienna narrowed her eyes. "I have a name," she said coldly.
"I am not invisi—"

Jesse's fingers bit into her elbow.

"You're here to take notes," he said in a low voice. "Not to
intrude or interfere. Got that?"

"Whatever you choose to call them, you should remember
that women who take notes and run themselves ragged for
men like you are not pieces of furniture."

"The last place you ran yourself ragged for a man like me was
last night, in front of the fireplace," he said even more coldly than
she. "And it was hardly an event I'd want to remember."

God, he was despicable! Sienna clamped her lips together
and followed him into a lush office. A football field long, at
least. Or damned close.

"Jesse," the small man behind the big desk boomed as he
shot to his feet, hand extended.

"Henley." Jesse shook the man's hand. Sienna waited ex-
pectantly. "My secretary," he said. No name. No look in her
direction. None from Henley, either.

Sienna gritted her teeth.

Jesse took a chair before the desk. Sienna looked around.
There was a straight-backed chair against the wall. Jesse looked
at her, jerked his head toward the chair. She marched to it.
Could you grit your teeth hard enough to dislocate your jaw?

"Coffee?" Henley said.

Jesse nodded. "That would be fine."

The small man looked at his secretary. "Coffee for Mr.
Blackwolf, tea for me." He chuckled. "I've had enough caffeine for the day."

"Oh," Sienna said brightly, "tea has as much caffeine as…"
They all looked at her. She cleared her throat. "Actually, I'd
prefer tea, too, if you—"

She was still speaking when the secretary left. Henley and Jesse chatted about this and that. Definitely, you could dislocate your jaw, so Sienna gave up tooth-grinding for lip-gnawing. She endured the serving of coffee and tea to the two men, took out a notebook, uncapped a ballpoint pen and prepared to take notes.

"...so," Henley said, "the bottom line is, I'm advising against buying this company."

"Your reasons?" Jesse said.

"There are many. First of all, my research indicates it's very risky. Who knows where computers are going to go?"

Sienna's head came up.

"Their use is surely limited. They're enormous. They require dust-free, air-conditioned rooms."

"There are personal computers out there already."

"Small, underpowered things, Mr. Blackwolf. My assessment is that they'll never find favor with any sort of substantial segment of the populace."

Sienna snorted. Both men looked at her. "Uh, sorry," she said. "I, ah, I sneezed."

Jesse narrowed his eyes, then focused on Henley again. "I appreciate your concern, but my understanding is that this company has a significant chance of surviving and prospering."

"The company is new. It's probably underfunded." The consultant shook his head. "It doesn't actually deal in computers, it deals in what's called 'operating systems.'" He flashed a pitying smile. "Trust me when I tell you that IBM has a lock on that market."

Sienna looked up. "Operating systems? IBM operating systems?"

Jesse flashed her a warning look. Henley ignored her.

"More to the point, the two men who started this company

are children, Mr. Blackwolf. Well, they're barely in their twenties. Neither has a college degree."

"I know, but I've done a lot of reading on Gates and Allen, and—"

"Paul Allen?" Sienna said. "Bill Gates?"

"Miss—Miss whatever your name is, if you would kindly—"

"Jesse. They're Microsoft!"

Jesse looked at her. "That's right."

"That's the company you want to buy?" She laughed. "You can't. But ohmygod, buy as many shares as you possibly can!"

"Really, young lady…"

Sienna got to her feet. "I am not a young lady," she said, "I am Mr. Blackwolf's administrative assistant."

Henley looked confused. "Isn't she your secretary?"

"Jesse," Sienna said, "this man's advice is dead wrong."

"Now, wait just a minute, miss! I am not going to permit a—a secretary to—"

"I told you, I'm not a secretary. I'm an administrative assistant. A personal assistant." The consultant flashed a smug, sexist smile. Sienna narrowed her eyes. "And you can get that look right off your face. That phrase does not mean what a sleaze like you thinks it means."

Henley shot to his feet. "How dare you?"

"How dare I not?" Sienna strode toward him and leaned across the desk, her nose inches from his. "You don't know what you're talking about when it comes to computers. Or me."

The man turned scarlet. He glared at her, then at Jesse. "Mr. Blackwolf. I am waiting for this young woman's apology."

Jesse gave a lazy smile. He stood up, held out his hand. "Thank you for your time, Henley."

"But we're not done here, sir! We have a great deal more

to discuss. I've taken the liberty of checking around. Have you considered the growth potential in Polaroid cameras?"

Sienna snorted again. The men looked at her. "I promise you," she said sweetly, "that was not a sneeze. It was a polite belly laugh."

"Listen here, Miss—"

"Cummings. Sienna Cummings. *Ms.* Sienna Cummings. *Miz*, not Miss. I assume you've heard the term."

"Well, that explains it. You're one of those—those bra burners who favor unisex bathrooms."

Sienna blinked. "Excuse me?"

"The ERA. The Equal Rights Amendment. I know your type. I just cannot imagine you, Mr. Blackwolf, employing someone like this."

Sienna and the attorney both looked at Jesse. His face was unreadable. *Oh, God,* Sienna thought, *after all he's done for me...*

"Jesse," she said unhappily. "Jesse, I didn't mean to—"

"Thank you for your time," Jesse said again. And he took Sienna's arm and hustled her to the door so fast that her feet almost left the floor.

He hailed a taxi as soon as they reached the street.

Sienna sat huddled in one corner. If only Jesse would say something—but he didn't. He gave the driver a destination and completely ignored her.

Moments later, their cab pulled up at a hotel at the top of a steep hill. Jesse stepped from the cab; she scooted out after him.

"Jesse," she said in a low voice, "I know you're angry but—"

"Evening, sir. Madam."

At least the doorman was willing to acknowledge her presence. Not that she cared. The only man whose acknowledgment mattered was Jesse.

Had she ruined an important business relationship for him? She'd certainly ruined his meeting. She hadn't meant to do either; she'd intended to do as he'd asked. Not interfere, not speak out, not intrude…

An elevator whisked them to the top floor of the hotel. They stepped out into a dazzling restaurant crowded with patrons. Was her boss going to feed her before he fired her?

Sienna tried again.

"Jesse. I'm sorry if—"

He put his hand on the small of her back. His touch was cool. Impersonal. Why did she want to lean back into it, turn that casual touch into a caress?

A smiling maître d'hôtel greeted them. "Good evening… Ah, Mr. Blackwolf. Welcome back, sir."

"Good evening, John. I'm afraid we don't have a reservation."

"No problem at all, sir. If you'd follow me, please…?"

The maître d' snapped his fingers. A busboy whisked a discreet "reserved" sign from a window table with an expansive view of the city. As soon as they were seated, the sommelier appeared and handed Jesse a drinks list.

He waved it away.

"A bottle of Krug *Grande Cuvée*."

The sommelier beamed with approval. Sienna didn't. Who cared about champagne right now?

Although, it would have been nice if Jesse had thought to ask her if she liked champagne… And what a petty thought at a time like this! She was lucky he hadn't ordered champagne for himself and hemlock for her.

"Look, Jesse, I know I was out of line, but I couldn't let that man talk you into making a huge mist—"

The champagne arrived. Sienna waited through the ceremony of Jesse examining the bottle, the sommelier expertly popping the cork, the presentation of the cork, the pouring of the sparkling wine so Jesse could taste it, then the pouring of it into two glasses.

She could feel her patience fraying. Such nonsense. Such an expression of male vanity. Men still did it in her time and it was just plain silly….

Damn it, so what? Explaining why she'd done what she'd done was what mattered.

She tried as soon as they were alone again.

"Jesse," she said urgently, "will you at least look at me? I can explain—"

"Thank you," Jesse said politely as the waiter handed them menus. Jesse looked his over. Sienna didn't bother. Reading a menu wasn't important right now, either. If only Jesse would say something…

"Sienna?"

At last! She breathed a sigh of relief. "Yes! Thank you for—"

"What would you like for dinner?"

Okay. It was mundane, but it was a complete sentence and he'd directed it at her. That had to be a good sign.

"The prime rib? Rack of lamb?"

She glanced at her menu, frowned and took a better look. Something about it wasn't…

"Hey." She looked up. "There's something wrong with this menu. It doesn't have prices."

Jesse gave her the kind of officious smile that had been a specialty of her third-grade teacher.

"Of course not. This is an expensive restaurant. They don't give women menus that show prices."

Her mouth dropped open. "Excuse me?"

"I said—"

"I heard what you said. Why don't they?"

"Well, because that's the way it is. A woman doesn't need to worry over trivialities. Now, what would you like?"

Sienna thought of a dozen different answers. Not one had to do with food…but, okay. She wasn't going to make a scene.

"The lamb. And a salad." The waiter appeared and she turned her attention to him. "Um, I'll have—"

"The lady," Jesse said, "will have the lamb. And a salad."

"How would madam like the lamb, sir?"

"Sienna?"

Maybe she really was invisible. "Madam," she said carefully, "would like the lamb done medium rare."

"Medium rare," Jesse repeated without missing a beat.

Sienna's eyes flashed. Good, Jesse thought, biting back a grin. She'd been the epitome of contrition ever since she'd shown up Henley as the jerk he was. It was nice to see some fire in her again.

"And how would madam like her salad dressed, sir?"

Jesse looked across the table. "How would you like your salad dressed?" he said politely.

Some fire? She was breathing fire. Jesse fought back the urge to reach out and pull her into his arms.

"Sienna? Your salad—"

"I would like my salad with oil and vinegar on the side," she said, the words directed at the waiter.

The waiter looked at Jesse.

"The lady," Jesse said, "would like her salad with—"

"You know what you need, Blackwolf?" Sienna's voice was low, razor-sharp and ice-cold. The waiter, clever man that he was, took a quick step back. "A new tape for that—that ancient eight-track of yours. *'I Am Woman.'* Ever hear it? *'I am woman, hear me roar!'"*

Jesse sighed. "Henley was right. You're a bra-burning feminist."

Sienna's chair fell over as she shot to her feet.

"That's it! I've had enough." She slapped her hands on the table, leaned forward and glared into Jesse's midnight-black, give-nothing-away gaze. "I was going to apologize for ruining your meeting. For speaking up. But why should I be sorry for behaving like—like a person?" She stood straight, turned her hot glare on the startled diners at the other tables. "Why should I apologize to anyone for not being a 1970s Stepford robot?"

Jesse shoved back his chair. "The check, please."

"That's it. Hustle me out of here. Get the—the silly little woman out of sight so she can't make a scene."

"Oh, there's no check, sir," the waiter said nervously. "None at all…"

"Let me tell you something, Mr. Macho. It won't always be like this. One day, you're going to have to make room for women in your—your tight little world. And when that happens—"

Jesse dumped a handful of bills on the table. "Thank you," he said to the waiter. Calmly, not hurrying, he clasped Sienna's elbow and marched her through the restaurant, to the elevator.

"And when that happens," Sienna said shrilly, "just remember that I was the woman who introduced you to the real world. To the next century. To women as—as people, not as—"

Jesse pushed her into the waiting elevator car.

"Shut up, Cummings," he said.

Then he yanked her into his arms and kissed her senseless.

CHAPTER ELEVEN

He'd meant the kiss to be soft and easy.

Okay.

Maybe he hadn't meant to kiss her at all.

But that performance this afternoon…the way she'd bristled at the sales clerk's attempts to make her conform to a look that was supposedly appropriate; her struggle to contain her anger at Henley's nauseating sycophants; Henley's indignation at being shown up for the idiot he was. And now, all that stuff in the restaurant, her refusal to be treated like a not-very-bright child…

How could he not want to kiss her?

But not soft and easy. Forget that. Forget everything but what he'd wanted all along. What she'd wanted.

What would finally happen between them.

The elevator reached the lobby. The doors slid open. He took his mouth from hers. She grabbed him and brought it back. He let her do it, let the kiss go on and on and to hell with the little delighted gasps and whispers around them.

When he lifted his lips from hers again, she gave a soft moan of protest. He clasped her shoulders and looked down into her eyes.

"Come to bed with me," he said in a low, rough voice.

"Yes," she said breathlessly, "oh, yes."

"Now. Here."

She looked around, gave a soft laugh. "Here?"

He took her hand, brought it to his lips. "Don't move from this spot," he told her.

It was an order. A command. And hearing it sent a bolt of excitement through her.

He was gone for only a few minutes. Then they were in a different elevator. His arm was tight around her waist. It was a gesture of possession so male, so basic, that she feared she might melt into him.

He drew her down a long hallway, to a pair of double doors. Inserted a key in the lock. The doors swung open. She saw a huge sitting room, bathed in the glittering lights of the city that stretched beyond a wall of windows. Then he shut the doors, turned to her and took her in his arms, lifted her into him, gathered her to him so that each racing beat of his heart and hers were one.

He kissed her and the world fell away.

"Jesse." She sighed, her breath mingling with his, and he took her mouth in a kiss so deep it had no beginning and no end, swept her into his arms and carried her through the opulent suite to the bedroom.

Like the sitting room, it glowed with the reflected lights of the city. He put her down, slowly, never letting her body escape the kiss of his.

He heard the hiss of her breath as his erection prodded her belly.

She was trembling, her breathing was fast. He kissed her again and again, traced the outline of her breasts with his hands. She wore a bra, a dress, a jacket. Still, he could feel her nipples against his palms as she gasped against his mouth.

"If this isn't what you want," he said, his voice urgent with need, "tell me now."

She moved against him, her hips undulating against his.

"I want *you*," she whispered. "You, Jesse. You. You…"

He framed her face between his hands. Kissed her. She returned the kiss and sucked the tip of his tongue into the warm depths of her mouth. It seemed impossible for his erection to grow harder but it did, and he groaned with the pleasure-pain of it.

He told himself to slow down. Slow down. They had all night. He drew back, just a little. Opened the buttons of her jacket one by one. Pressed his lips to the hollow of her throat, felt the hot gallop of her blood beneath his mouth.

The jacket fell to the floor.

The outline of her breasts was clear through the clinging silk of her dress. He cupped them, feathered his thumbs over her straining nipples, exulting in her sharp little cries of pleasure. He was driving her crazy and driving himself crazy in the process, but it was worth it to hear those cries, to see rosy color stain her cheeks.

The dress closed with buttons. Small ones, damned near too small for his big fingers. He wanted to tear them apart, but even more, he wanted to prolong Sienna's pleasure.

He undid them carefully, but halfway down, he could take no more. He had to feel her naked skin, so he slid his hands inside the open bodice of the dress, felt the coolness of the silk, the heat of her skin, and gloried in the sensuous contrast.

"Jesse," she murmured, lifting her face to his.

He looked at her. Saw the glitter of desire in her eyes, the way her pupils had widened until only a rim of violet was visible around them. Her hair was loose and wild and incredibly sexy. Her bra was cream-colored lace, the darkness of her nipples shadowed like the outline of the sun in eclipse.

"Sweetheart," he said thickly, "you are so beautiful...."

Her hands rose, framed his face. She brought his mouth to hers, kissed him, nipped his bottom lip. He felt a fever rising inside him, the need to take her, possess her, mark her as his.

He growled, tore the dress from her shoulders. She moaned, nipped his lip harder as the fragile silk fell away.

Mercifully, the bra had a front closure. It gave way easily and then her breasts tumbled into his hands.

Sienna cried out. Whispered his name. Put her hands over his, held his hands to her. He dipped his head, kissed her throat, the sweet juncture of neck and shoulder.

Her hands fell away. Jesse looked at her. His heartbeat stumbled.

She was so beautiful. So feminine. So perfect.

He told her so, his voice hoarse with emotion, watching her face as he stroked her pale pink nipples. A sob rose in her throat; his name trembled on her lips and he bent his head to her breasts.

To the tightly furled tips.

He licked her flesh. Tasted it. And when she cried out again, he sucked at one sweet bud while he caressed the other.

Her moans became a keening cry of ecstasy. Her knees buckled. Jesse caught her, captured her mouth with his, held her close as he tumbled onto the bed with her in his arms.

"Jesse." Sienna was sobbing. Panting. Her lips were parted, swollen from his kisses. "Jesse, please, please, please..."

Her words, her yearning cries, fractured what little remained of his self-control. He stripped away the rest of her clothes, rose from the bed and tore off his. Then he came back to her, to her open arms, her soft mouth, clasped her wrists and drew her arms high over her head.

There was nothing gentle in him now. All of it had been consumed by his fierce need for her.

Only for her.

And she reveled in his hunger, matched it with her own, arching toward him, seeking his tongue, his heat, his passion. His lips moved over her, down and down and down as she writhed against him, aching for his possession.

"Please," she said again, and he reached out, found his jacket on the floor, found one of the little packets he'd bought in the hotel pharmacy. He tore it open with his teeth, rolled on the condom and then he moved between her thighs, his swollen sex brushing against her. She was hot and wet, the exquisite proof of how badly she wanted him. He let go of her wrists, slipped one hand under her bottom, spread the other over her, his palm against her weeping flesh, watched her face, saw her eyes widen, heard the long expulsion of air as he parted her, sought her clitoris, stroked it...

She screamed. And he...he was going to explode if he didn't end this torment.

"Sienna," he said, "my Sienna..."

And he thrust deep, deep inside her.

She cried out, shattered instantly. Somehow, he held back. Stayed hard. Stayed buried inside her and moved again. And again. And again until he thought he might die of the pleasure of it, until he felt her womb starting to convulse around him.

"Look at me," he demanded.

Her eyes flew open, met his as her second orgasm tore through her.

"Jesse," she whispered, and he knew that was what he'd needed. His name on her lips as he claimed her body, her soul...

Her heart.

Jesse flung his head back and soared with her into the moonlit night.

Minutes later, hours later, Sienna drew a long, shaky breath.

Jesse was sprawled over her, his face buried against her throat. Her arms were wrapped around him, holding him to her. His skin was damp, as was hers; their racing heartbeats seemed to be slowing in unison. The scent of him—sinfully sexy, musky and male—was in her nostrils.

She didn't realize she'd whispered his name until he stirred and pressed a kiss to her shoulder.

"I know, baby. I'm too heavy for you—"

"It isn't that. I just…I just like saying your name."

He kissed her collarbone; she felt his lips curve in a smile.

"And I love hearing you say it. But I'm still too heavy for you."

Her arms tightened around him. "Don't go. Not yet."

"I'm not going anywhere. Not without you. I'll be right back, I promise."

He rose from the bed, went into the adjoining bathroom. Seconds later, he came back to her, gathered her so that he held her in the cradle of his arms, their bodies touching, their faces inches apart. He smiled into her eyes, lay one hand against her cheek in a caress so gentle it made her throat constrict. She turned her head and kissed his palm, and he angled his head above hers and gave her a soft, lazy kiss on her mouth.

"You okay?"

She nodded. "Yes."

Another tender kiss. "I wasn't too fast?"

"You were wonderful."

He flashed a sexy grin. "All compliments noted and happily

accepted, ma'am." Slowly, his smile faded. "What's wonderful is you."

"Jesse." She felt her cheeks flush with color. "I've never—I mean, I've never before felt—"

"No," he said softly, "it's never been like that for me, either." He dropped another soft kiss on her lips. "I feel as if I've known you for a hundred lifetimes."

Two, anyway, she suddenly thought, and shuddered as the sudden coldness of reality intruded.

Jesse rose on one elbow, frowned and searched her eyes with his.

"Baby? Baby, what's wrong?"

"Nothing. I just—I just…" She took a breath. "What's that old saying?" she said with forced lightness. "Something about a goose walking over my grave."

He grinned. "No gooses here. Just me."

As he'd hoped, that made her laugh. "It's geese."

"Nope," he said, deadpan, "not a one. No gooses and no geese, either. The only other critter here is me."

Sienna batted her lashes. "Well, yes. You. And me, of course. But…" Her hand slid between them. His breath caught and she smiled. "But then, there's this."

In a heartbeat, Jesse had rolled her onto her back.

"Be careful, woman," he said in a teasing growl, "or be prepared to pay the price."

"What price would that…? Oh. Oh, God, Jesse…"

A second raced by while he sought another condom, sheathed himself again. Then he wove their fingers together, held their hands at their sides as he entered her.

"Here's the price," he whispered. "This. Always this."

Always, she thought… But how could there be an "always" for them?

Sienna let their passion sweep away the sudden despair that threatened to destroy her.

It was dark when Jesse awoke.

"Sienna?"

She was gone. The sheets, the pillows, still held her scent, but he was alone in the bed.

Fear clawed his throat. He rose quickly, pulled on his jeans, hurried through the dark suite…and saw a bright light beyond the sitting room.

He paused, blew out a breath and asked himself just what was he doing, feeling as if the earth had given way under his feet because a woman he barely knew might have slipped from his bed.…

And his life.

Ridiculous. They'd slept together, that was all. He wasn't looking for involvement. What for? Life was simpler without it, neater and cleaner and…

And, he walked into the pool of light, saw Sienna seated at the white marble counter, wearing an oversized terry-cloth robe, her face buried in her hands, heard the muffled sounds of her sobs, and he knew he was the greatest liar on this lonely planet.

Life might be simpler without involvement, but it was also meaningless.

"Baby," he said, and went to her, and even as she said "No, don't, just leave me alone," he was taking her in his arms, she was spinning toward him, winding her arms around him, weeping as if her heart were about to break.

He crooned soft words to her. Stroked her hair, her shoulders, her back. He gentled her as he would have a filly in desperate need of a tender touch, and after a while, her sobs eased.

Her grip on him did not.

Carefully, he lifted her from the stool, carried her into the sitting room, settled into a big chair with her safely in his lap.

"What is it?" he said. "Sienna, sweetheart, talk to me."

She shook her head, kept it buried against his chest. He cupped her cheek, urged her face to his. Her hair was wild and tangled, her eyes were violet pools of sorrow, her nose was pink and running. She was beautiful beyond belief, and with stunning suddenness, he knew that finding her had changed his life forever, that what he felt for her went beyond passion and desire.

It scared him almost as much as it filled him with joy, he thought, and he gathered her even closer.

"Don't cry," he said. "Baby, please. Tell me what it is. I'll make it better. Just tell me."

"I can't."

"Yes, you can. Whatever it is, sweetheart, I promise, I'll make it better."

She gave a sad little laugh. "But you can't. No one can make it better. If I were to tell you—if I were to tell you about me…"

Hell. She was talking about why she'd come to the canyon. The sacred stone, the ledge, all that nonsense that didn't mean a damn to him anymore, that could never, even when he'd bought into it, mean half as much as she did.

"Sienna. There's nothing you could tell me that would change how I feel about you."

"I know you believe that, Jesse. But it's not true." She took a deep, shuddering breath. "There are things—there are things about me that would—would change everything."

"No," he said emphatically. "I don't believe that."

"Jesse." Gently, she put her fingers over his lips. "Either you wouldn't believe me or you'd—you'd see me differently, see me as someone else, someone you thought you knew but didn't, and—and—"

He kissed her. Kissed her until her mouth softened under his, until she was clinging to him. Then he rose to his feet with her still in his arms, carried her back to the bedroom, pulled the duvet from the bed and wrapped them both in its voluminous folds. French doors opened onto a terrace. He opened the doors, carried her outside, sat in a wicker chair with her in his arms.

"Warm enough?"

She nodded. How could she not be warm in Jesse's arms? The cold would come soon enough, when she told him what she should have told him much, much sooner. That she wasn't of this time, of his time. That somehow she had stumbled backward more than three decades.

And delaying things wouldn't make the telling any easier.

Sienna looked at her lover's face, so strong and proud and beautiful in the moonlight.

"All right." Her voice was low. She took his hand, clasped it tightly in hers. "Here's what you need to know about me. And—and it really will change what you think you feel about—"

He kissed her to silence. When he lifted his head, he looked deep into her eyes.

"I know what I feel about you," he said softly. "And nothing can change it."

Her eyes filled with tears. "I'm not—I'm not who, I'm not what you think I am."

"I don't give a damn about that," he said, almost angrily. "Whatever you've done, why you were in the canyon…" He brought her hand to his lips. "It's history."

She laughed, even as she wept. "No. It isn't history. It's just the opposite. But you have to know the truth, and—and the truth can change things."

"Yes. You're right." He took a long breath, slowly expelled it. "And that's why you need to know the truth about me."

"No. Jesse—"

A muscle flexed in his jaw. He lifted her from his lap, carefully tucked the duvet around her, got to his feet and walked to the terrace railing, his strong, half-naked body outlined by the lights of the city far below.

"I told you that I was in Special Forces. You know what that means?"

She nodded. Of course she knew. Even in her world, people spoke with awe of the Green Berets, soldiers who fought clandestine battles. They were the bravest of the brave.

"And you know about this war." His mouth twisted as he turned toward her. "This goddamned war that's finally come to an end."

Bewildered, she stared at him. The wars in the desert kingdoms? He couldn't be talking about—

"Vietnam," he said, almost spitting out the word. "A politicians' war—paid for with the blood of men like the ones with whom I served."

Vietnam. Of course. She knew of it, that it had been unpopular, that in her time, not his, the men in suits who had directed it from the safety of their comfortable offices had finally acknowledged it had been fought wrong.

"They died because of me," Jesse said, his voice so low she could hardly hear it. "Because I was fool enough to order them to do things when I knew it was all wrong, that what we did didn't really mean a damn, that there was no way to win."

"No! Jesse, you did what you were ordered to do—"

"Men died because of me. Soldiers. Warriors. Men? Damn it, they were kids! I didn't stop it, couldn't stop it—"

Sienna rose in one fluid motion and went to him.

"Jesse. Sweetheart, listen to me—"

"You think it's okay. But it isn't. It changed everything. I've seen how some people look at me. I've heard their whispers." A long, deep breath. "My wife laid it all out."

Sienna went rigid. "You have a wife?"

"I *had* a wife. She left me, we got a divorce. The marriage wouldn't have lasted, anyway—it was one of those things, a mistake, from the beginning. We'd dated in high school. I came home from college, we went out a couple of times... And I enlisted."

"You enlisted," Sienna said softly. She put her hand lightly on his arm, felt the terrible tension in his muscles. "Jesse. Whatever you did in the war... You were a hero."

He shook his head. "I was a fool," he said bitterly, "all fired up on nonsense about warriors and honor and fighting for what was right."

She moved in front of him, rose on her tiptoes and kissed him. "You *are* a warrior, Jesse, and a man of honor who fought for the men beside you."

He looked at her then, saw the glitter of tears in her eyes. They were for him, and though he had shoved away Linda's initial offerings of polite sympathy, he knew Sienna's tears were more than that. They were tears of compassion, of caring...

Of caring, he thought, and his heart seemed to lift inside him.

"It's cool out here," he said softly. He put his arm around her, plucked the duvet from the terrace floor where it had fallen and led her into the bedroom. "Come on, sweetheart. Let's see if this place has the fixings for tea. Okay?"

She nodded. "Okay," she said as she burrowed against him.

In the kitchen again, he found a kettle, tea bags, mugs, spoons… He kept busy, fidgeting with them, arranging them, and then, when there was no arranging left to do, he turned to Sienna, sitting at the counter.

"We got married for all the wrong reasons." The kettle whistled. He unplugged it, poured the boiling water into the mugs. "She, because she thought I was somebody I'd never wanted to be. Me because, I don't know, it seemed the right thing to do." Jesse put a steaming mug in front of Sienna. "It didn't take long to know we'd screwed up. We tried, for a while. She wanted a bigger house. I tore down the old one and built a new one. It didn't matter. She said I was a stranger." He gave a hollow laugh. "Hell, I was. To her, to myself."

Sienna waited. When he said nothing, she touched his hand. "And?"

"And, my marriage was finished, my folks were gone, everything I'd believed in seemed meaningless. I decided to start over. Numbers had always been my thing. When I was a kid, math was the only subject I bothered with. When I got older, it was poker." A quick smile tilted his lips. "I'd played cards in Saigon and Tokyo and what seemed like half the army bases in the civilized world, came home with a lot of money, decided stocks were more interesting than poker." His jaw tightened, his voice went flat. "I made even more money, bought this place. But it didn't change anything. I was still me, inside."

"And that's why you're going to sell your land," Sienna said softly.

He nodded. "It's not a good place anymore. Too many memories, you know? The nonsense my old man fed me about a warrior's vows, a warrior's obligations…" Silence. Jesse put down his untouched mug of tea and took Sienna's hands in his. "Then, one night, I rode out into Blackwolf Canyon. I told myself it was so I could say a mocking goodbye to the past."

He reached for her hands and brought them to his lips. "And," he said, with a simplicity that brought tears to her eyes, "I found you. A miracle, waiting just for me."

Sienna wanted to put her arms around him, this brave, wounded hero, this amazing man, this lover who had stolen her heart. But she couldn't, not until he knew everything.

"Jesse. What you said about how the truth can change things…"

His eyes grew dark. She could see him withdrawing from her emotionally even as he let go of her hands.

"It's all right. I understand. You don't have to ex—"

"Damn it," she said, her voice ragged, "do you think anything you just told me could change what I feel for you?" She grabbed his hands, held on tight. "It's the truth about me that will change everything." She drew a deep breath, expelled it, then looked directly into his eyes. "I'm not a thief. I'm not some leftover sixties flower child."

"I know that, baby. Besides, I told you, whatever, whoever you are—"

"I'm Sienna Cummings," she said, hurrying the words because if she didn't, she knew she'd lose courage. "I live in Brooklyn, go to school in New York City. I'm a graduate student in anthropology at Columbia University." She stopped, voice and body shaking. "And two days ago, when I first set foot in Blackwolf Canyon…"

Oh, God! She couldn't do this but she had to, it was time, it was past time….

"Sweetheart?"

Sienna wound her fingers tightly through his.

"Two days ago, when we met… Two days ago, Jesse, the year wasn't 1975. Not for me. For me, it was—it was the year 2010."

CHAPTER TWELVE

SHE'D stunned him.

No surprise there.

How else could she expect him to react when she'd pretty much said, *I'm not a thief, not a late-model hippie, what I am is a woman from the future.*

Maybe a better description was that Jesse looked like a man waiting for the punch line to a bad joke.

"The year 2010," she said. "That's thirty-five years from now. Well, thirty-five years, fourteen hours and—and—" She looked at the face of the small clock on the wall. "And I'm not really sure how many minutes. Unless you figure in the time difference between here and Mont—"

"We need to get you to a doctor."

"No!"

"Yeah. We do." Jesse's voice was rough, filled with urgency. "Which is better? To see someone here or in Montana? Montana. I know people there—but this is a big city. Lots of hospitals and doctors and—"

Sienna shot to her feet. "A doctor will put me away! And I'm not crazy. I'm not, I'm not, I'm—"

Jesse cursed. Grabbed her. And kissed her. Kissed her hard,

kissed her deep, as if the force, the power of his kiss could chase away demons.

Or could, at last, finally force him to acknowledge the truth.

He had refused to admit that truth these past years. Hell, he'd denied it much of his life. Now he had to face what he'd always somehow known.

For all his anger, all his defiance, some of the old ways were true.

Why hadn't he seen it from the start? The ledge. The sacred stone. The solstice. The green lightning. And Sienna, suddenly appearing where nobody had been before. The truth had been staring him in the face, but he'd been too pigheaded to see it.

"I'm not crazy," she said in a shaky whisper when he took his lips from hers, and he gave a gruff laugh and drew her against him.

"No, baby. You're not."

She raised her head and looked up at him. There was such certainty in his voice….

"I should have known," he said. "Right from the minute I first saw you."

"I don't understand."

"The sacred stone…" He framed her face with his strong, work-roughened hands. "My father told me stories, sweetheart. Ancient stories about what could happen on that ledge when the sun or the moon was just right."

She stared at him. "You mean—you mean, others have—have…?"

Her knees turned to rubber. It was one thing to assume you'd traveled through time and another to hear someone say that you had. She felt herself falling, heard Jesse say her name. Then she was in his arms and he was carrying her through the suite, to the bed where he lay her gently back against the pillows.

"I was right," he said, sitting beside her, taking her icy hands in his. "You do need a doctor."

"No! Please, no doctor. Didn't you just say that I'm not—I'm not—"

He kissed her. Tenderly. Sweetly. A sigh trembled on her lips as he drew her head against his shoulder and enfolded her in his strong arms.

"You're not, sweetheart. But you've been through one hell of an experience. I just want to be sure you're all right."

"I will be," she said, drawing back and meeting his eyes, "once I understand what happened."

Jesse looked at her lovely face. How could he have known her for, what, just a couple of days? He felt as if he'd known her all his life. As if he'd known her forever.

And maybe he had. Maybe the old stories weren't stories at all.

"Jesse. Please, tell me about the ledge."

"I don't know all that much."

"Whatever you do know, then. Tell me."

Eyes steady on hers, he told her some of the stories he'd been raised on. "Fairy tales, you know?" he said, smiling a little. "The Rabbit and the Elk. *Unktomi*—the Spider—and the Arrowheads. An Indian kid's version of Hans Christian Andersen."

She nodded. "Legends. Myths. Ancient tales passed from generation to generation."

"My beautiful anthropologist," he said softly.

That made her smile. At least some of the wild darkness was fading from her eyes.

"My dad was a scholar, as well as a rancher. He taught me all kinds of stuff about his people."

"Your people," Sienna said softly, touching a hand to his cheek.

He caught her hand and kissed it. "That's what my mother would say, when I got into my teens and began scoffing at the stories. 'These are your people, too, Jesse,' she'd tell me. And the truth was, I loved the stories—especially the ones that were really outrageous. Stories about that ledge. The sacred stone. And shamans."

"Wise men who could perform feats of magic."

"So the stories claim."

His tone was cynical, but Sienna understood. She'd always held such beliefs in great respect, but to believe in them, to believe in the supernatural…

"Go on," she said softly.

"The stories hinted at a kind of hole in time, an emptiness that could draw life in."

"And?"

Jesse shook his head. "That's all I know," he said softly.

Sienna nodded. She bowed her head. Her shoulders slumped. He cursed, reached for her and drew her into his lap.

"I wish I knew more," he said, "but I don't."

"That must be what happened to me." Her voice wobbled. "It sounds impossible, but there's no other explanation."

"No," he said gruffly, "there isn't."

Her eyes filled with tears. His arms tightened around her. He was a man of action. A soldier. You saw something happening, you reacted. You did what needed to be done.

Except for this.

What did a man do to comfort a distraught woman? He'd have moved mountains if it would have taken away his Sienna's tears. He'd never felt so helpless in his life.

"You must feel lost," he said softly, and then an awful thought struck him. "Sienna? Is there somebody—would someone be looking for you back in your time?"

She shook her head. "My parents are both gone. I have a couple of cousins somewhere, but I haven't seen them in years."

"Nobody else?"

This time, she heard the hidden question behind the simple words and she put her hand against his cheek.

"Nobody else," she said softly.

Jesse drew Sienna closer and rocked her in his arms.

"Everything will be okay," he said. "I'll take care of you. I promise."

She shook her head. "I don't want to be a burden to you. You didn't ask for this mess—"

"Is that what you call it when a miracle drops into your life?" Slowly, he raised her face to his, kissed her eyes, her lips. "You're the best thing that's ever happened to me, sweetheart. I'll do whatever it takes to make you happy."

"You're what makes me happy," she whispered, and knew, with all her heart, that was the truth.

Only a son of a bitch would feel good, hearing something like that, but if that was what he was, so be it. Jesse drew Sienna closer and rocked her in his arms.

They went back to his apartment in early morning, stopping first to buy fresh sourdough rolls and freshly ground coffee from a little shop nearby.

"I'll show you the city after we have some breakfast," Jesse said...but somehow, they never made it out the door. They never even made it to breakfast. Instead, as soon as they were alone in his place, Jesse phoned his housekeeper, told her to take a few days off...

And carried Sienna to bed.

But, as she laughingly pointed out, food was also one of

ife's necessities. So, in the late afternoon, they showered,
ressed and went out to see San Francisco.

Day after day, the city showed itself to be a lovers' paradise.
The charming little restaurants. The steep hills. The cable
ars. Little places that served dim sum in Chinatown, the
moky coffee houses of North Beach…

It was almost enough to make a man and a woman forget
hat she had come here in a way neither of them understood.
And when that wasn't quite enough to keep the truth at bay,
being alone together in Jesse's big, wide bed surely was.

It was, Sienna was certain, the most perfect place in the
world to lie in your lover's arms. To tremble with passion as
he entered you. To fall into dreamless sleep and then come
awake to his slow, deep moonlit kisses or to the hot, sun-
inged stroke of his hands.

She had never been this happy in her life. Jesse was—he was
wonderful. Good and kind. Exciting and sexy. He was everything she'd ever hoped a man could be, a complex mass of con-
radictions and juxtapositions that were absolutely amazing.
He knew how to leave a mass of salesclerks swooning in his
wake after an afternoon of nonstop, far-too-expensive
hopping and then cap it off by buying her a tacky and adorable
tuffed toy from a street vendor whose pitch made her laugh.
He could confer with the snootiest sommelier as easily as he
could get lunch at a hot-dog stand. And, as she quickly learned,
he was fine with letting her choose what she wanted to drink
and eat, and in ordering them without his help.

And when she figured out that he'd deliberately baited her on
their first evening in the city, she called him an awful man and
uined the effect by flinging herself into his arms and kissing him.

Her Jesse was, yes, wonderful.

And all at once, looking at him one morning over late coffee in his sun-filled apartment, Sienna felt as if the earth had suddenly tilted under her feet.

She was in love with him.

The cup in her hand trembled. She put it down and tried to tell herself it wasn't true. She couldn't have let that happen. Loving Jesse was a dangerous, foolish thing. Bad enough she'd become his responsibility, but to love him, to want him to love her when passion, not love, was on his agenda...

"Sienna." Jesse rose from his chair and came quickly to her side. "Baby, what is it?"

"Nothing. I'm—I'm fine."

"The hell you are." He drew her chair back, lifted her to her feet. "You're not happy."

"Jesse—"

"With me? Or with being here?"

"Oh, no, it isn't you! It could never be—"

"Do you miss 2010?" His jaw tightened. "Do you wish you could go back?"

He had never asked her those questions. And she hadn't given them much thought. At first, she'd been too busy trying to accept what had happened, but yes, at the beginning, if there'd been a way to return to her own time...

"The only place I want to be is right here."

Jesse felt as if he'd been holding his breath. "Good," he said gruffly. "Because we're going home."

"Home?"

"To Montana. It's where I really belong. And where I want—where I want you to be with me."

"Are you sure? I mean, I can get a job here, you know? Find a place to live—"

Jesse silenced her with a kiss. It was a long, tender kiss; he felt her holding back, and then, gradually, her lips softened clung to his, and when he finally lifted his head and looked into her eyes, he felt as if a blindfold had been torn from his eyes.

Somewhere between the sacred stone in the wild beauty of Blackwolf Canyon and this very unsacred high-rise in the sophisticated beauty of San Francisco, everything in him had changed. And Sienna was the reason.

He was in love. Deeply in love, for the very first time in his life.

Was it too soon to tell her that? Would she want to hear it? She'd gone through so much in such a short time....

"Jesse." Her voice was a husky whisper. "Do you mean it? Do you want me to—to be with you?"

He threaded his fingers into her hair, lifted her face to his. Maybe she needed some breathing room. He could say he was offering her a safe place until she decided what to do next—

But lying to her was impossible.

"Yes," he said gruffly. "I want that more than my next breath."

She rose on her toes and kissed him. It was a kiss filled with all the promise a man could want. He drew her against him, returned the kiss, took it slow and deep and hot until she moaned into his mouth.

Then he undressed her. Touched her. Drew her onto a chaise longue where he followed each stroke of his hand with a stroke of his tongue and when they were both half crazy with hunger, he entered her.

And knew he wanted her to be his, forever.

They flew back to Montana that evening.

Home, Jesse had called it, and that was the way it felt to Sienna, but then, what was it someone had once said? Home was where the heart was. And her heart was here, with Jesse.

The year could be 1975. It could be 2075. It could be anything, just as long as she was in his arms.

He was everything she had ever dreamed a man could be. Strong. Tender. Gentle. Fierce. He was her beautiful, macho warrior.

And she adored him.

He introduced her to his men. They were true sons of the Old West, courteous and gallant in their dealings with her. At Jesse's urging, his foreman selected a gentle chestnut mare for her; one of the younger hands brought her a hand-made bridle and shyly said he'd be honored if she'd accept it.

Jesse stood by, grinning with pride.

Mornings, they both worked, he on the ranch, she on its books. Afternoons, they rode the land together. He took her to the ancient sites shown him by his father, sites he had so recently derided. To his delight, Sienna already knew most of them. She had studied this place, learned the Blackwolf secrets.

But one secret remained. Jesse's secret. That he loved her.

He longed to tell her, but how? Instinct told him the moment had to be right. Sienna understood the old ways. He wasn't sure he respected them anymore, but she did….

And with that realization, he had the answer to his question.

Two nights later, he went to the safe in his office. Took out a bracelet, very old, made of braided horsehair with a sterling-silver-and-pipestone clasp. His father had given it to his mother; his grandfather had given it to his grandmother. Men of his tribe had given the bracelet to the women they loved for more generations than he could count.

Tonight, he would give it to his Sienna.

They ate supper before the living room fireplace, steaks he grilled and a salad she put together in a wooden bowl. His father had carved it, he said with pride. She smiled. It was easy to see he had loved his parents, that he loved this place, this land...

"Are you really going to sell this place?" she suddenly said, her promise not to mention the sale cast aside.

He looked at her. He'd all but forgotten the papers in the folder on his desk.

"Years from now, someone is going to turn it into a resort."

He nodded. "Sooner than that," he said, "but not really a resort. A group of homes on big chunks of property, maybe a ski lift."

Sienna shook her head. "The land will remain untouched until 2010. Then a developer will fill your beautiful canyon with row upon row of houses built around a golf course."

The muscle jumped in his jaw. A week ago, he wouldn't have cared. At least, that was what he'd told himself. Who gave a damn for ancient rituals, for the sanctity of the land? He'd wanted to rid himself of a burdensome past filled with lies about honor, duty, history.

Now that had changed. A woman, this woman, had brought him back to himself. He could no more sell the land of his fathers than he could give her up, and he smiled as he took her into his arms.

"I won't sell this land," he said softly. "How could I, when it brought me you?"

Hours later, an enormous white moon began rising in the black velvet sky.

Jesse stirred, rolled on his side and stroked a gold curl from Sienna's forehead. "A full moon," he said softly. "Will you come out on the porch and see it with me?"

She sat up. The beautiful old quilt from the sofa dropped

to her waist, revealing her breasts. He cupped one, caressed the sensitive tip, watched her eyes darken.

"The moon will be beautiful," he said in a husky whisper, "though not as beautiful as you."

Sienna brushed her lips over his. "Can we see it from the canyon?" She smiled. "It would be the perfect end to a perfect day."

She was right. Still, he felt a quick sense of unease. And that was nonsense. The canyon was as much his home as this house. Hadn't he just thought of how it had brought Sienna into his life?

"Jesse?"

He kissed her. Her mouth, her throat, her breasts. "You'll have to pay the price when we get back."

Her soft, sexy laughter made his body harden in anticipation.

"You drive a tough bargain, Mr. Blackwolf."

The dark mood that had threatened to overcome him fell away. He rose to his feet, pulled on his shirt, his jeans, felt the outline of the sterling-pipestone-and-horsehair bracelet in his pocket. Smiling, he offered her his hand.

"Come on, woman," he said in a teasing voice of command. "We're wasting time."

She rose in one sinuous motion. The darkness hovered over him again, but he told himself he was being an idiot, and he flashed a grin and swatted her on her naked backside.

"Hey," she said, with mock indignation.

He tilted her chin up and dropped a light kiss on her nose.

"I'll saddle the horses while you get dressed."

"Perfect," she said.

She was right. What better place to give her the bracelet than the canyon where they'd found each other?

What better place to tell her that he loved her, and wanted to make her his wife?

CHAPTER THIRTEEN

THEY rode out slowly, the horses casting long shadows as they picked their way over the meadow.

The night was still and cool, the sky a black colander pierced by the light of a thousand stars. A fat ivory moon rose above the jagged rim of the canyon, limning the stark peaks with an almost merciless light.

It was beautiful, all of it. The moon, the stars, the canyon and Blackwolf Mountain, now looming just ahead...but Jesse's feeling of unease was growing.

Maybe coming out here hadn't been such a good idea.

Halfway into the canyon, he reached for the mare's reins and brought both horses to a halt.

Sienna looked at him in surprise. "Why are we stopping?"

Why, indeed? He, of all people, didn't believe in premonitions. Besides, he wasn't having a premonition, he just had this uncomfortable feeling...

"Jesse? I thought we were going to ride all the way into the canyon, to Blackwolf Mountain."

He draped Cloud's reins over the saddle horn and slid to the ground.

"The view is perfect here," he said, reaching up to Sienna.

"See? The stars, the moon right overhead…" He smiled as she slipped into his arms. "Besides," he said, "it's been too long since I kissed you."

She laughed softly as she linked her hands behind his neck.

"Much too long," she agreed, and lifted her face to his.

He kissed her, his mouth gentle on hers, tasting the sweetness that was hers alone, gathering her tightly to him until their bodies seemed to be one. Somewhere in the distance, a coyote sent a mournful cry into the night.

Sienna shivered.

"Baby? Are you cold?"

"No. It's just…" She hesitated. "There's such a sense of peace here, but there's also—there's something else. I don't know how to describe it. It's just a feeling—"

"Yes. I know." He did. He felt it, too. An indescribable sense of peace and—and something more, something that made the hair rise on the nape of his neck.

It was as if the canyon was filled with the old beliefs tonight. Nonsense, of course. Besides, he'd brought Sienna here for a reason. This was where he had found her. It seemed right that this should be where he told her how much he loved her.

"Sweetheart?"

"Mmm?"

"I have—I have something to tell you."

She tilted her head. "Something bad?"

Great. Just great. That was one hell of a start, but then, he'd never done this before. He and Linda had just sort of ended up married; he'd never been able to remember actually proposing.

The coyote howled again—or was it a coyote? The sound was too deep, too wild, too filled with loneliness. Sienna caught her breath.

"Jesse, that's a wolf! I didn't know there were wolves left in Montana. There will be, in my time, but not now."

"Yeah. It's a wolf, all right. I've seen him. A big guy. A male."

"Ah," she said, the word filled with compassion. "He must be lonely."

Jesse nodded and raised her face to his. "He is," he said quietly. "He needs a mate. A mate he can love, who will love him forever."

His voice was low. Sienna's heart began to race.

"What a lucky female she'll be."

He smiled. "You think?"

"I know. To have a mate like that…"

"Sienna. I'm in love with you."

She didn't move. Didn't answer. His gut knotted. Why hadn't he waited? It was too soon. She wasn't ready. She might never be ready. Maybe what she felt for him was gratitude.

He was a fool. He was moving too fast, asking too much of a woman who was still trying to understand what had happened to her—

"Oh, Jesse…"

He swallowed hard. "Yeah. I know. Too much, too fast, too—"

"Jesse, I love you, too. I adore you!"

Jesse whooped as if he were a warrior counting coup. He'd learned the victorious cry from his father, passed it on to the men he'd led into battle—and had never imagined making such a joyous sound again. Sienna laughed as he caught her in his arms, whirled her in circles and kissed her, over and over.

When he put her on her feet, their laughter stopped. He looked deep into her eyes.

"I have something for you," he said softly. "I know I've told you I don't believe in the old ways, but…" Moonlight lit the bracelet as he took it from his pocket. "But I believe in this."

Sienna caught her breath. "Oh, it's beautiful."

"It's old. Very old. My father gave it to my mother. His father gave it to his mother. The men of my father's family have given it to their women for hundreds of years." He paused. Sienna's eyes were on his. What was she thinking? She'd said she loved him, but another woman, one to whom he'd never given this bracelet, had once used those same words…

"I know what it is," she said softly. "It's a totem. A token." She reached out and put her hand on his chest. "And I am honored that you offer it to me."

Jesse felt his throat constrict. "But?"

She gave a low, quicksilver laugh. "But, if you don't say the rest of the words, I'm never going to forgive you!"

It was as if all the pain, all the despair in his heart gave way.

"The honor is mine," he said as he slipped the ancient bracelet on her wrist. "Sienna. Will you marry me and be my love, forever?"

Tears glittered in her eyes. "Oh, yes. Yes, my darling, yes!"

Jesse gathered her close, bent his head and kissed her. Her lips parted under his; the taste of her filled him. He slipped his hands under her sweater, groaned as she sighed her pleasure into his mouth.

Thunder, deep and menacing, rolled across what had been a cloudless sky.

Sienna jumped. "Jesse?"

He looked up. What the hell was happening here? The moon was suddenly gone. The stars had fled. The canyon had become so dark that he couldn't even see the horses. Through the impenetrable blackness, he heard Cloud's terrified whinny.

"Jesse." Sienna wrapped her arms more tightly around him. "What's going on?"

It was a damned good question. He didn't know, didn't like not knowing. Something nuzzled his shoulder. Cloud, he thought with relief, and grabbed for the reins with one hand.

"Come on," he said grimly. "Get up on Cloud and we'll get the hell out of—"

The thunder rolled again. It sounded like a freight train aimed directly at them. Sienna screamed—and, all at once, a shaft of green lightning split the darkness.

"Jesse!"

He dropped the reins, gathered Sienna more closely against him. Something—the wind, the night—something was trying to tear her from his arms.

"I've got you," he shouted. "I won't let you go—"

It didn't matter.

One second, the woman he loved was in his arms.

The next, she was gone.

The low buzz of voices.

A warm breeze.

Cool water on her face.

Sienna moaned. "Jesse?"

"She's coming around," a voice said.

"Thank goodness!" another voice added.

"Sienna? Open your eyes."

It wasn't easy, but she did. And moaned again. Her head ached. She was nauseous. Dizzy. And the sun, beating down on her, was a brutal force.

The sun?

Oh, God! "Jesse," Sienna gasped, and sat up.

"Easy."

The voice was male—but it wasn't Jesse's. She blinked; faces came into focus. "Jack?"

"Take it easy," Jack said. "Don't try to move just yet."

"What happened?"

"We had one of those crazy summer electrical storms," one of the grad students said excitedly. "Lightning, you know? It hit too close and you passed out."

"Jesse," she said again, her voice trembling.

"There's no Jesse here," Jack said impatiently.

"She must have been dreaming," the grad student said.

Sienna raised a shaking hand to her head. There was a lump behind her ear. "What—what happened?"

"We just told you," Jack said, his tone accusatory.

"A storm," the grad student said. "And a bolt of what looked like green lightning hit the ledge up there."

"And," Jack said, "you went down."

Sienna stared at him. "So—so, I was unconscious?"

"Yup."

"But—but for how long? How many days?"

Jack snorted. "Days? Minutes, just minutes. Ten. Fifteen. Something like that."

A moan burst from Sienna's throat. A dream? Was that what this had been? Only a dream? No. No!

"You were out long enough to miss the good news."

"What good news?"

"Just had a text message from the university. We can take our time with this expedition. Turns out the land's not for sale, after all."

Sienna felt her heart lift. "It isn't?"

"Nope. Somebody just found papers dated July '75. Seems the guy who owned it changed his mind, turned the place into a trust that'll stay forever wild."

Sienna's head was spinning. If she'd dreamed it all, why had someone just found papers making the canyon and the surrounding land forever wild?

And yet—and yet, such a thing was feasible. Lawyers and scholars were always turning up old documents.

But she couldn't have dreamed Jesse. He had been so real. His kisses. His smile. His love.

Tears rose in her eyes. She dug in her pocket for a tissue, found none and wiped her arm across her face.

"Hey," Jack said, "nice!"

She blinked. "What?"

"Never noticed that before." She looked at him blankly. "The bracelet. Must be a few hundred years old. Didja get it in Bozeman?"

Sienna looked at the beautiful bracelet that encircled her wrist. Horsehair. Sterling silver. Pipestone.

"Jesse," she whispered.

Her heart filled with joy. What had happened had been real—but it was over. She had lost Jesse, she would never lie in his arms again.

Burying her face in her hands, she began to weep.

"What?" Jack said, but she didn't even try to answer.

After a while, they all walked away. Trauma, she heard one of them say. Stress.

Let them think what they wished. There was no possible way to explain what had happened…

Or to explain her broken heart.

Time slipped past.

It didn't rush backward or gallop relentlessly forward. No holes swallowed Jesse up. Time just kept moving, and so did he.

He spent days searching the canyon, the mountain, every

inch of his land, looking for Sienna, even though he damned well knew he wouldn't find her.

Something had torn her from his arms. Something more powerful than any enemy he'd ever encountered. This was an enemy he could not see, could not describe, could not touch.

Could not defeat.

The realization half-killed him.

His woman was gone. God only knew where she was, and he—he was helpless to find her.

His men treated him with caution. They thought Sienna had left him. He didn't try to explain. How could he? He couldn't explain it to himself.

When he ran out of places to search, he flew to San Francisco, to New York, to half a dozen universities where scholars knew all there was to know about astronomy and time and physics. When he ran out of universities, he walked the streets of dangerous neighborhoods, sat through the nonsense of séances and tarot-card readings. He was willing to try anything, everything.

It did no good.

Sienna was gone.

It was his fault.

If only he hadn't brought her to the canyon…

He tried not to waste time on self-pity. All he wanted was to figure out what had happened, come up with a way to find his Sienna and bring her back.

Was she in her own time again? Maybe. He tore up the sale papers for his land, had his bewildered attorney draw up documents that would instead protect it forever.

Maybe she would know about it.

It was like putting a message in a bottle and tossing into a vast, uncharted sea, but it was, at least, something.

And, finally, when there was nothing else left, he buried himself in work. He sweated and toiled alongside his men, rebuilding fences, herding, branding, doing whatever he could to keep from thinking of what had been taken from him forever, what he would never find again.

Days became weeks, weeks became months. The heat of summer gave way to the chill of autumn. Winter was fast approaching. The weather, like Jesse's heart, was cold and bitter.

Nights were the worst. You couldn't do much on a ranch once darkness settled over it. He took to going through the old books and papers his father had collected.

Maybe, just maybe, he might discover something in them that would help him understand what had happened.

The books were full of legends. The papers were mostly notes that spoke of things Jesse no longer believed but could not so easily dismiss, not after what had happened to him and the woman he loved.

Then, one night, he stumbled across a map. It was old, older than the bracelet he'd given Sienna; it had been drawn on a piece of tanned deerskin. It took less than a minute to see what it depicted: the canyon, the ledge, the sacred stone.

A sheet of paper was clipped to it. Jesse recognized his father's handwriting.

The old ones believed the passageway above the sacred stone was more than an entrance for the summer sun. Some believed it was a portal between worlds, that when proper conditions existed, one could travel through time.

Jesse's heart began to race. He sat down at his desk and read the rest. At first, the words erased any faint hope he might have harbored. Some ancients had apparently gone through the opening between the stones to another time. None had ever come back.

But every four hundred years, his father had written, there would be a very special summer solstice. It was said that on that day, one chosen by fate could slip through the opening. The portal would remain open until the sun could no longer climb to the top of Blackwolf Mountain. Then, months later, at the moment when the shortest day became the longest night, it would close and remain closed until the four-hundred-year cycle repeated.

The moment when the shortest day became the longest night. When the shortest period of daylight became the longest period of darkness.

The winter solstice.

"The winter solstice," Jesse said, and leaped to his feet.

Today was December 22. The winter solstice would happen today. Or tonight. Who knew what you called that precise instant that marked the dividing line between the shortest number of daylight hours and the longest time of darkness? All that mattered was that the winter solstice was coming, and yes, all this old stuff was rubbish…

Except, maybe it wasn't.

Maybe it was real. Hell, of course it was real. How else could Sienna have come to him? She had been the one chosen by fate to slip through time. He had no idea why, didn't give a damn why…

He only knew that it had happened.

Could that honor somehow now fall to him?

What could he lose by trying?

"Nothing," he said into the silence of the room. Nothing, when he had already lost the only woman he would ever love.

He looked at his watch. It was already going on eleven. It sounded like a bad joke, but he was running out of time.

What did a man take when he hoped to travel through time? He grabbed his wallet, ran for the door, stopped, went back and scooped up the envelope confirming his ownership of Microsoft stock that had come in the day's mail, stuffed everything into the pocket of the denim jacket he grabbed from a hook in the mudroom. He headed for the barn. The Silverado would be faster but instinct told him a horse, not a truck, was the right choice for what would surely be the most important ride of his life.

He didn't bother saddling Cloud, simply slipped on the stallion's bridle, then jumped on his back and leaned over the proud, arched neck.

"Go, boy," he whispered. The horse seemed to sense his urgency. Cloud tore over the land, across a thin layer of icy snow, the frigid wind blowing in Jesse's face.

But he'd made a mistake. Riding the stallion had seemed right, but even Cloud's great speed had not been enough. By the time they reached the canyon, the demarcation between autumn and winter was less than two minutes away.

Jesse slid from the horse's back and ran toward Blackwolf Mountain, looming high above him. He looked up at it; the darkness was so deep he couldn't see the ledge. He couldn't see anything, not the stones, not the handholds he'd need.

"Sienna," he said, his voice rising into the silence of the night like a prayer. "Sienna, I love you, sweetheart! Sienna!"

All at once, thunder roared eerily overhead. Echoed over the mountain. Lightning, green as an emerald's heart, sizzled through the black winter sky.

Jesse flung back his head, threw up his arms.

"The old ways can never die as long as they live in your heart," he cried. "I was too foolish to see that until now!"

The lightning struck. He felt as if his soul were on fire.

"Sienna," he whispered.

The lightning struck again and he fell, unconscious, to the ground.

Sienna had vowed never to return to Blackwolf Canyon.

It held too many memories that broke her heart.

She'd buried herself in work, going on digs in Mexico and in Belize. She'd explored sites no one had seen in thousands of years, unearthed pottery that now was on exhibit in the great American Museum of Natural History in New York. She'd written endless papers. She had her doctorate.

But nothing would ever fill the void in her heart.

She lived in Manhattan now, in a small apartment near the museum. And dreamed, every night, of Jesse, awakening each morning with her pillow damp with tears.

But this morning was different.

She awoke very early, and with a sense of anticipation. It made no sense. This would be a day like any other. She'd work all day, come home to an empty apartment and tumble into bed, exhausted, to dream again of all she had lost.

The only thing different was that this was the morning of the winter solstice.

"So what?" she said into the silence.

The answer came with stunning speed.

Sienna. You must be in Blackwolf Canyon at midnight tonight.

Wonderful. Now there were voices in her head.

It was crazy and she wasn't going to do it. Hadn't she vowed she would never go back? But the voice inside her was persistent, and finally she stopped trying to figure out if maybe, this time, she actually was going crazy. There was only one way to find out.

She rushed to Kennedy airport, went to the American Airlines ticket counter and said she had to be in Bozeman, Montana, by evening.

There was one ticket available; it took her to Denver, where she changed planes. Once in Bozeman, she rented a Jeep, drove like a madwoman across the wild, empty land with Blackwolf Mountain on the horizon first as a speck, then a dot, then as a towering presence.

When she finally drove into the canyon, it was eleven o'clock. She put her foot down on the gas pedal until the Jeep was damned near airborne.

She had to reach the mountain, reach the ledge; she had to be there when the shortest daylight hours of the year became the longest hours of darkness even though she didn't know why….

And, God, she wasn't going to make it. The dashboard clock read three minutes to midnight.

"Come on," Sienna said, her voice shaking, "come on, come on, come—"

Thunder roared overhead. She cried out; the Jeep skidded on the icy grass as the thunder roared again. There it was. The mountain, a dark, menacing hulk straight ahead.

Lightning, green lightning, slashed the sky.

Sienna stood on the brakes. Flung open the door. Her lips were moving in silent prayer. She didn't know what it was, what she was saying, only that she wanted the green lightning to strike again, to hit her squarely as she raised her face and arms to the sky.

It struck.

Not her.

It struck all around her and she screamed as the world tilted….

"Sienna?"

Her heart stood still. That voice. That beloved voice, husky and deep and so wonderfully, magnificently familiar.

The sky lightened. The moon appeared. The stars, a billion of them, blazed down on Blackwolf Canyon….

"Sienna," Jesse said, and when she spun around she saw him running toward her, arms open and waiting.

"Jesse? Oh, God, Jesse!"

She flew into his embrace, weeping, sobbing, tasting the salt of their commingled tears as they kissed. He held her that way for a long, long time and then, at last, she drew back and looked up into his beautiful face.

"How?" she whispered.

He shook his head. "I found something my father had written. And I knew, I just knew it meant I could find you." He lifted her off her feet. She wrapped her arms around his neck and buried her face against his throat. "Never leave me again," he said fiercely.

"Never. Never, never, never…"

He kissed her. She clung to him. Suddenly, a big, velvet muzzle intruded between them.

"Cloud," Jesse said, and laughed. The stallion whinnied; gently, Jesse pushed him away. "I love you, Sienna," he said softly. "I always will."

"Until the end of time," she whispered.

"Until the end of time," he echoed, because as long as he had this woman in his arms, time had no end. The year, the place didn't matter.

Jesse Blackwolf was, at long last, home.

MILLS & BOON®
are proud to present a new series

n o c t u r n e ™

Three dramatic and sensual tales of paranormal romance
available every month from June 2010

The excitement begins with a thrilling quartet:

TIME RAIDERS:

Only they can cross the boundaries of time; only they
have the power to save humanity.

The Seeker by Lindsay McKenna
21st May

The Slayer by Cindy Dees
21st May

The Avenger by PC Cast
4th June

The Protector by Merline Lovelace
18th June

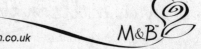

millsandboon.co.uk Community

Join Us!

The Community is the perfect place to meet and chat to kindred spirits who love books and reading as much as you do, but it's also the place to:

- Get the inside scoop from authors about their latest books
- Learn how to write a romance book with advice from our editors
- Help us to continue publishing the best in women's fiction
- Share your thoughts on the books we publish
- Befriend other users

Forums: Interact with each other as well as authors, editors and a whole host of other users worldwide.

Blogs: Every registered community member has their own blog to tell the world what they're up to and what's on their mind.

Book Challenge: We're aiming to read 5,000 books and have joined forces with The Reading Agency in our inaugural Book Challenge.

Profile Page: Showcase yourself and keep a record of your recent community activity.

Social Networking: We've added buttons at the end of every post to share via digg, Facebook, Google, Yahoo, technorati and de.licio.us.

www.millsandboon.co.uk

2 FREE BOOKS
AND A SURPRISE GIFT

We would like to take this opportunity to thank you for reading this Mills & Boon® book by offering you the chance to take TWO more specially selected books from the Modern™ series absolutely FREE! We're also making this offer to introduce you to the benefits of the Mills & Boon® Book Club™—

- **FREE home delivery**
- **FREE gifts and competitions**
- **FREE monthly Newsletter**
- **Exclusive Mills & Boon Book Club offers**
- **Books available before they're in the shops**

Accepting these FREE books and gift places you under no obligation to buy, you may cancel at any time, even after receiving your free books. Simply complete your details below and return the entire page to the address below. You don't even need a stamp!

YES Please send me 2 free Modern books and a surprise gift. I understand that unless you hear from me, I will receive 4 superb new books every month for just £3.19 each, postage and packing free. I am under no obligation to purchase any books and may cancel my subscription at any time. The free books and gift will be mine to keep in any case.

Ms/Mrs/Miss/Mr _____ Initials _____

Surname _____
Address _____
_____
_____ Postcode _____
E-mail _____

Send this whole page to: Mills & Boon Book Club, Free Book Offer, FREEPOST NAT 10298, Richmond, TW9 1BR

Offer valid in UK only and is not available to current Mills & Boon Book Club subscribers to this series. Overseas and Eire please write for details.. We reserve the right to refuse an application and applicants must be aged 18 years or over. Only one application per household. Terms and prices subject to change without notice. Offer expires 31st July 2010. As a result of this application, you may receive offers from Harlequin Mills & Boon and other carefully selected companies. If you would prefer not to share in this opportunity please write to The Data Manager, PO Box 676, Richmond, TW9 1WU.

Mills & Boon® is a registered trademark owned by Harlequin Mills & Boon Limited.
Modern™ is being used as a trademark. The Mills & Boon® Book Club™ is being used as a trademark.